THEY CAME TO TUCSON

Cooper Dundee—Wild and rough as the territory he traveled, he would not yield his hold on the Dundee stage line and ranch without a fight—even if it would tear his family apart.

Jonathan Dundee—Beneath his fine clothes and refined talk he was a bitter calculating schemer who would betray his father's legacy and risk full-scale war to build his own career.

Regan O'Rourke—A fiercely capable investigator, she found herself trapped in the ugly and violent quarrel between the Dundee men. One she trusted and respected—and came to fear. The other she started out despising, but came to need—and love.

Ramón Delgado—A vindictive and unforgiving man, he led a band of misfit mercenaries to terrorize the Anglo settlers he hated.

The Stagecoach Series
Ask your bookseller for the books you have missed

STAGECOACH STATION 12:
TUCSON

Hank Mitchum

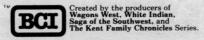

Created by the producers of
**Wagons West, White Indian,
Saga of the Southwest,** and
The Kent Family Chronicles Series.

Chairman of the Board: Lyle Kenyon Engel

BANTAM BOOKS
TORONTO · NEW YORK · LONDON · SYDNEY

STAGECOACH STATION 12: TUCSON

*A Bantam Book / published by arrangement with
Book Creations, Inc.*

Bantam edition / June 1984

*Produced by Book Creations, Inc.
Chairman of the Board: Lyle Kenyon Engel.*

ISBN 0-553-24126-5

Published simultaneously in the United States and Canada

PRINTED IN THE UNITED STATES OF AMERICA

O   0 9 8 7 6 5 4 3 2 1

STAGECOACH STATION 12:

TUCSON

ARIZONA TERRITORY 1879

PRESCOTT

DUNDEE TRANSPORT

PHOENIX

Salt River

CASA GRANDE

Gila River

DUNDEE RANCH

YUMA

SOUTHERN PACIFIC R.R.

PICACHO PASS

SITE OF O CAMP GRANT MASSACRE 1871

TUCSON

FORT LOWELL

San Pedro River

Santa Cruz River

© BOOK CREATIONS INC. 1983

RON TOELKE '83

Chapter 1

Prescott, Arizona Territory, lay wasting beneath the August sun. Cooper Dundee, part owner of the Dundee Transport Line, stopped and looked up from his chores of polishing the brass and oiling the woodwork of the old, carefully preserved stagecoach that was brought out once a year for the special run from Prescott down to Tucson.

The special run—which took the Arizona territorial representatives back to their homes in and around Tucson after the legislature adjourned each year—was always nostalgically taken in the original Dundee Transport Line stagecoach.

The old desert craft had survived the years well. She had stood the test of time with the grace of a *grande dame* well skilled in the subtle artistries of makeup, the minor flaws that had come with age adding character to her bearing. Even the gilt trim that adorned the panels seemed to complement the weather-worn lacquer, catching the sunlight and holding its brilliance to form bright, glowing halos against the dark woodwork.

Twin landscapes were painted on the single doors at each side of the coach. The clear oils Cooper smoothed across the scene renewed the vibrant whites and silvers of a frosty New England snowscape, the ice-covered lake shimmering against a backdrop of snow-dusted pines and white-capped mountains. In the heavy heat of an Arizona morning, the frozen lake seemed even more enticing, and the man's fingers lingered longer than he intended.

The still morning air suddenly came alive with the high-pitched shrieks of small children, whose rough-and-tumble antics churned up great clouds of yellow dust from the un-paved street as they raced across the wide thoroughfare to attack Cooper from the rear. His surprise seemed genuine, and soon the man's rich baritone mingled good-naturedly with the jubilant screams of the youngsters.

Gallantly, Cooper Dundee fought the good fight. He chose to prolong the skirmish, knowing that in the end he would surrender, and he covered his head with both arms in an attempt to suppress the laughter. The troop of young boys piled on top of him and pinned him to the ground. Straddling him—one on each arm and leg, and two more who bounced up and down on his belly and chest—the half-dozen children shouted in one voice, "Say 'uncle'!"

Cooper convulsed in laughter, bucking away from small, tickling fingers. And then, thoroughly winded, he succumbed. "Uncle," he breathed. When nothing happened, he repeated the word much louder. *"Uncle!"* Slowly, cautiously, the motley crew unwound themselves. One by one, they gave up their places, rising to stand in a tight but ragged circle around the man.

He pulled himself erect, stretching to his full six feet two, the handsome product of his Scotch father and Indian-Mexican mother. He was a lean man, a year past thirty, his sun-bronzed cheeks contrasting sharply with the amber-flecked green eyes that dominated his face. Dark hair, untouched by the sun, fell across his high forehead, the sweat-damp locks at his neck and ears tightly curled. He swore softly, raking his fingers through the unruly mop, and stooped over to pick up his hat.

The flat-crowned, wide-brimmed plainsman hat seemed his only concern now, and he was fastidious in his attention to the numerous dents and creases that pocked the battered felt.

Lovingly, he patted the Stetson back into shape, rotating the hat in a slow circle around his bent elbow as he dried the sweatband on his sleeve. Finally satisfied, he settled the hat squarely on his head, the wide brim shadowing the laughter in his eyes.

The game then resumed when ten-year-old Toby Udall swaggered forward, properly insolent as he played out the charade. An old sombrero hid his thick head of red hair, while his freckled nose and grubby chin were covered with a bright red bandanna. He cocked his head and stared up at Cooper, his eyes narrowed in an expression of unspoken menace.

More threatening than his sneer was the fearsome weapon he was now pointing at Cooper's belt buckle. In his small boy's mind, his mother's discarded broom became a long-barreled Sharps rifle, the stubby straw nub firmly pressed against his right side. He palmed back an imaginary hammer, cocking the piece and poking it at Cooper's belly with great authority. "Your money or your life, pilgrim," he growled. The large cinnamon jawbreaker that nested in his fat cheek was now a chaw of tobacco, and he worked it against his jaw until he collected just the right amount of the pungent juice. Forcing a cough, he spit into the dirt between Cooper's feet. "You heard me, mister," he drawled. "Your money or your life!" The five similarly armed outlaws at his back echoed his demands.

Outnumbered, Cooper offered no resistance. He began a frantic search of his pockets, his outer vest pocket first and then his trousers. Slowly, he probed the depths of the right front pocket, pulling it inside out to a chorus of whispered dismay. The make-believe road agents moved closer, watching as the man flicked away imaginary pieces of lint in his fruitless search for treasure.

At last, as the band of midget marauders inched closer, he plunged his hand deep inside the remaining pocket and delved to the very bottom. There was the faint jingle of coins, more

prolonged hesitation, and then—as he withdrew his hand—
the bright flash of copper.

He doled out the coins until each small hand held its own
Indian-head penny, and then, aware of an additional pair of
eyes beyond the circle, he produced yet another. He tapped
Toby's shoulder and pressed the second coin into his palm.
"For your friend," he smiled, nodding toward the porch.

Michael Patrick O'Rourke stood in the shadows on the
wood-plank sidewalk in front of the Dundee Transport Line
office, far apart from the others. More than distance separated
him from the boys in the street. The distinct eastern cut and
style of his factory-tailored suit as well as his unnatural
tidiness set him apart.

His coat was of dark navy velveteen, with elaborate cord
piping forming ornate frogs that fastened around glistening
black buttons. Matching knee pants topped spotless white
stockings, and on his feet were a pair of patent leather shoes.
A yellow straw topper banded with a navy blue ribbon perched
on his dark head, the black hair intensifying the flush of
embarrassment on his pale cheeks. He shifted uncomfortably
under the mass scrutiny, his blue eyes begging for acceptance.

Toby Udall snorted disdainfully. He handed the extra coin
back to Cooper, contemptuous. "Him?" he scoffed. "That
army brat ain't no friend of mine." He was remembering his
mother's gossip about the ten-year-old orphan boy from nearby
Fort Whipple. "Cholera," she had said. "His ma and pa—
everybody but the boy dead from cholera. And him with no
one but an old maid aunt he's never seen to raise him. . . ."

Facing the boy, not caring about his troubles, Toby stuck
out his tongue. "Look at him! He's a baby," he mocked. "A
baby and a sissy."

His words were picked up by the others, and they chanted
them over and over in a soft singsong: "Baby, baby,
ba-a-by . . ." The object of their ridicule glared at his tormentors, anger painting his cheeks a bright red.

Cooper pushed his way through the barrier of children, his

eyes on the child on the porch. The boy was miserable, and that misery showed plainly on his face and in his posture. He was nervously chewing on his bottom lip, and his small button chin was trembling. The youngster's fists were knotted at his sides, and suddenly, without warning, he yielded to his growing temper and charged across the walkway.

"Whoa, partner!" Cooper caught the boy. Holding on, he hunkered down, his eyes exploring the youngster's face. He relaxed his grip, loosening the taffeta tie at the boy's neck. "A little hot for this, isn't it?" The jacket was next, then the patent leather shoes. "These, too," he said softly, lifting first one foot and then the other as he removed the cotton stockings. He stuffed the stockings and tie into one sleeve of the coat, and then set about loosening the boy's wide, starched collar. "Bet you a dollar your ma made you wear this." He straightened up before the boy could answer, his hand still resting comfortingly on the youngster's shoulder.

The teasing chant stopped, and the band of children moved closer. Their appraisal was less critical than before, but the wariness and inborn need to dominate their own territory and its people were still there. In spite of the subtle change in appearance, the boy on the walkway was still an outsider.

"You know him, Coop?" Toby edged nearer, until he was nose to nose with Michael. *He's so prissy clean,* he thought scornfully and reached out, smudging Michael's shirtfront with his dirty thumb and forefinger.

Cooper felt the youngster tense as Toby touched him. "Sure," he lied. The answer did little to appease Toby's suspicions or to soothe the beginnings of his gnawing jealousy. Cooper sensed the need for something more, so he turned his newfound ward around until they faced each other. "Tell you what, partner. . . ." A silver dollar appeared in the man's hand as if of its own accord, and he rotated it slowly between his thumb and forefinger. There was a round of covetous "ohs" from the others, and Coop smiled. "Why don't you let Toby here show you where the biggest and best candy jar in all of Prescott is kept?" He folded Michael's fingers around the coin and winked. Then, almost as an afterthought, he removed the boy's straw hat and replaced it with his own.

Michael's face colored and split open in a smile that threatened to push his ears clear around his head. Toby's matching smile was just as gregarious. He let out a joyous whoop and, grabbing Michael's hand, led a wild, thumping charge down the wooden sidewalk.

Retreating before the thundering horde was Estevan Folley, who backed up in mock horror, wisely pushing himself against the red brick wall at his back. The children pounded by him, their bare feet and exuberance combining in a great force that reverberated through the dry planking. The boards rose and fell beneath him, and Estevan felt the bobbing sensation of a man adrift in a small boat.

The same age as Cooper—and like his best friend, also of mixed Anglo and Spanish blood—Estevan was a territorial representative who was returning to his home near Tucson now that the legislature had adjourned. Although young and brash, Estevan had been elected by his constituents because his mixed heritage and outspoken honesty brought him everyone's trust. He stood for a time, watching as the pack of children disappeared into the mercantile, and then turned his attention back to Cooper.

"Tell me, friend," he began, pausing as he tried to check his laughter, "did the girls over at Cory Paxton's whorehouse decide it was time all their whelps got acquainted with their papa?"

Cooper turned at the sound of the familiar voice, his green eyes warming. "Hell, no, *compadre*," he drawled. "She kept my twelve at home but sent your six over here to make sure you didn't sneak out of town without paying your bill." He shook his head, smiling as he gestured with outstretched arms. "Eminent territorial legislator," he scolded, "she claims you've got a tab this long. . . ."

Folley snorted, his dark eyes, so like those of his Mexican

mother, measuring the considerable distance between Cooper's hands. "It wasn't my *tab* she was talking about, fool," he boasted.

Cooper's reply was lost in a sudden explosion of good-natured laughter. He reached out, wrapping his arms around his friend in a massive bear hug. "You better peddle that line of bull somewhere else, old son! You're talking to the man who had to show you how to relieve yourself standing up!"

They stepped back, and Folley regarded his friend closely. "It's been a long time, Coop." He hesitated, considering his words carefully, and began again. "I'm sorry about your father, Coop," he said softly. "I was in Washington when I heard Malachai had died, and when I got back . . ." He shrugged, words failing him.

Cooper nodded, understanding the awkward silence. He picked up the cloth that was hanging on the porch railing and stepped back down into the street. It was almost a year since his father had died from a riding accident, and the pain was still there, prolonged by his stubborn refusal to believe that Malachai's death had been accidental—as well as the reluctance to accept the fact that his father was dead and that he was now one-third owner along with his mother, Teresa, and half brother, Jonathan, of the stage line.

The sweet scent of lemon and paraffin oil permeated the air as Cooper resumed his chores. He reached out, rubbing the finish on the leeward door of the coach, losing himself in the solitude of the painted lake.

His daydreams were interrupted by the scratch of a match against the iron-bound rear wheel. Estevan was leaning against the yellow-rimmed wheel, his head bent forward, blue-white smoke churning the air as he sucked deeply on a brown-papered cigarillo. He offered the smoke to his companion. "Beitermann and the other legislators didn't think the line would be making the special run this year," Estevan finally said.

As Cooper inhaled on the cigarillo, he gave the door

another swipe, stifling a cough as the smoke invaded his lungs. "Malachai made this run every year since '63. There's no need to end it, just because he's gone."

Folley had the distinct impression that Cooper was talking about something more than the annual trip the elder Dundee had initiated the year Arizona first became a federal territory. "So you're making the trip with Jonathan's blessings," he ventured.

Cooper laughed and took another drag on the small cheroot. When he realized that he had been hogging the smoke, he handed the butt back to his friend. "Of course I have big brother's blessings!" he lied. Seeing the concern on Estevan's face, he reached out and placed his hand on the man's shoulder. "Jonathan and I have learned the noble art of compromise, Mr. Representative," he teased. "Give a little, take a little. Hell, he's even agreed to hire some outside help to get the line back on its feet!" The half-truth had the hollow ring of a total lie, and Cooper knew it. The reality was that Jonathan had hired an efficiency expert from the East—one Mr. Regan O'Rourke—to verify his belief that the company would continue to operate in the red, despite any efforts.

Folley finished the smoke and ground it under his heel. He had heard of Jonathan's efforts to find someone impartial to assess the line's present status, just as he was aware that the real purpose of the assessment was to clear the way for an anticipated sale. There was no tactful way to say it. "Word is that the line is up for sale, Coop. Word is Jonathan has already found a buyer."

"No!" There was a vehemence, a poorly restrained fury in Cooper's hasty answer. He took a deep breath, wishing he had another smoke, craving the sedative effect of the small cigars. Contrite, he raised his hand in a sign of peace, sorry that his inner rage had been directed at his best friend. "We're not going to sell," he said finally, shaking his head when Folley tried to interrupt. "*I'm* not going to let Jonathan sell."

Estevan searched his vest pocket for another smoke, sorry that Cooper's playful mood had dissipated. He knew how much the stage line meant to the man, what it represented. Yet in his practical, politician's mind he saw the futility of the dream. The railroad had already reached Prescott, and it wouldn't be long before Arizona Territory—north and south—was serviced by a fully operational line, a plan that already had the support of the majority of the legislature. "You know, Coop," he began, watching his friend's face and trespassing in a way no one else would dare try, "sometimes in order to gain something, you have to let go of something else. . . ."

Stubbornly, Cooper shook his head. He'd heard all the arguments and was tired of them. "Malachai was right about holding on to the stage line, Estevan. Just like he was right about refusing to sell the rights of way to Montgomery and his crowd." He could almost hear his father whispering in his ear: *They'll start their own stage line, run at a loss until they put us out of business, and then double their rates. And then they'll build their damned railroad and charge the people even more.* "Malachai was right," he said again, "and I don't give a tinker's damn if Jonathan and his speculating friends here—or anywhere else—think otherwise." He forced a smile, the anger beginning to tear at him again. "I don't want to talk about this, *compadre*. Not now."

The gentle rustle of starched cotton broke the awkward silence, the delicate scent of lavender spicing the quiet air. Together, both men turned to face the sound, neither of them able to conceal his surprise.

The woman was regally tall and unashamed of her height. Raven-black curls with a will of their own framed her alabaster face, and the pale skin and high cheekbones were dominated by a pair of incredibly blue eyes that seemed, to Cooper, somehow familiar. Only the downturned mouth spoiled the picture.

Instinctively, Cooper reached for his hat, the gesture fruitless as he remembered that he had given it to the boy. He turned the movement into a clumsy attempt to smooth his shaggy hair. "Ma'am," he greeted.

Out of the corner of his eye, he could see Estevan straightening from a properly polite bow, the man's dark eyes shining with appreciation at what he was seeing. "Estevan Folley, senora. At your service."

Smiling, the woman returned Estevan's greeting with a discreet nod. "O'Rourke," she said firmly, extending her hand. "*Miss* Regan O'Rourke."

There was an audible rush of air as Cooper exhaled, the sudden whispered *"Damn!"* louder than he intended. The woman's frown returned, and she measured him from head to foot, her long inspection making him uncomfortable and totally conscious of his disheveled appearance. She spoke again, her voice still soft, but the tone different. "I assume, *sir*"—the last word was more an expression of reproach than respect—"that you are the driver. . . ." She waved her hand at the coach.

Cooper answered quickly, before Estevan had a chance to make a formal introduction and explain that Cooper Dundee was one of the owners of the line. "That's right, ma'am." He smiled, warmly, the gesture as futile as trying to thaw a keg of ice with a single match. The woman's expression changed not one mote.

Instead, she turned her gaze on the small watch that was pinned above her right breast. She lifted it away from the pale-blue dress and tapped the crystal with a single, carefully manicured nail. "It's nine fifteen. This coach was to have been hitched, loaded, and ready to leave at precisely nine o'clock." There was a long silence as she waited for some response, and when it failed to come, she continued. "It's not difficult to see why Mr. Dundee finds it necessary to reassess the operation of this business. Between the obvious disorder in *there*" —she indicated the office at her back with a curt toss of her head— "and the lackadaisical attitude of the employees out *here* . . ." The disdain was evident again—in her words and, more plainly, in her face.

Estevan's hand covered his mouth. His words to Cooper were muffled, intentionally covert, his tone conveying his surprise. "Jonathan's efficiency expert," he whispered. He coughed, as if clearing his throat, and stepped forward, intent on correcting the woman's obvious misconception. "Miss O'Rourke . . ."

Cooper held him back, his hand on the man's sleeve. "The passengers," he interrupted, addressing the woman. "I'm still waiting for the rest of the passengers. . . ."

Regan's right foot was tapping impatiently against the porch flooring, small puffs of white dust rising to disappear beneath the hem of her skirt. "Perhaps if someone had bothered to post a schedule, you wouldn't have to wait." Her eyes scanned the barren chalkboard that hung precariously from a single nail on a post.

Cooper's tone matched the woman's, the sarcasm growing. "Just another example of our lackadaisical attitude, Miss O'Rourke. One more thing you can mention to Mr. Dundee."

The woman had a note pad in her hand, and the pencil seemed to fly across the page. "You can be sure that I will," she retorted, "at the same time I report your obvious disregard for your personal appearance while on the job." She raked his long frame with her eyes, pausing just long enough to take a deep breath. "I should say that Dundee Transport will definitely benefit from my having had to come to Prescott on family business rather than going directly to Phoenix. This has given me additional insight as to your incompetence—and the hundred or so miles between here and Phoenix will no doubt prove equally instructive. Oh, yes, I intend taking this stage to Phoenix—and beyond, should Mr. Dundee think it necessary. And I intend to leave within the hour!" She watched as Cooper came to attention, his heels snapping together sharply. The mock salute was militarily precise and intentionally arrogant. There was a brief flash of anger in the woman's blue eyes, and then an icy calm. "I mean it, Mr. . . ."

". . . Cooper," he finished. "Just Cooper."

She dismissed him, turning her back on him and heading back into the office. Midstep, she stopped. "Michael?" She called the name softly, urgently, as she spied the cast-off jacket and shoes and bent to pick them up. "Michael?" she repeated.

Cooper exchanged a quick glance with Estevan; it struck him why, when he first saw the woman and first looked into her blue eyes, she had seemed so familiar. "Your boy . . ." He knew immediately from the way her back stiffened that he had made a mistake, but it was too late to make amends. "He's with the others."

She spun around, the bundle of clothing clutched to her breasts. "The others . . . ?" The concern that had paled her cheeks was gone, replaced by a sudden flush of annoyance. "My *nephew* has been ill," she seethed. "Extremely ill." She had seen the other children from the window, had fleetingly watched the driver indulge them in their rough and tumble brawling. "He was supposed to be resting, Mr. Cooper. Resting! Not running the streets with some gang of hooligans and would-be thieves!"

Cooper closed his eyes, angry at her judgmental denouncement of the children and clenching his teeth in a supreme effort to keep his words civil. The apology that he had intended making hung bilious and burning in his throat. *You are a royal pain in the butt, lady,* he thought. Aloud, not caring anymore if he offended her or not, he said, "I gave him a dollar and told him to go find the biggest candy jar in town and have himself a real tear." He didn't know why the woman riled him so much, but there was immeasurable delight to be achieved in setting her off. "He looked as if he needed it," he finished.

She responded in kind, more quickly than the man expected. "Aha!" she proclaimed. "Stage driver extraordinaire, financier to the deprived, and now a physician!'' The dark curls haloing her face danced provocatively as she tossed her head and turned her eyes back on the small jeweled pendant at her breast. The watch rose and fell in perfect rhythm to her breath. ''One hour, Mr. Cooper. With or without the passengers.'' She lifted her eyes and stared directly into Cooper's, her voice lowering. ''With or without *you*. That coach is leaving for Phoenix in precisely one hour!''

Properly chastised, the man nodded. He watched as the woman departed, holding his tongue until she was well on her way down the sidewalk. ''You better get Beitermann and the others, Estevan. Like the lady said, with or without, that coach is leaving here in exactly one hour.''

Estevan's brows knotted. ''You should have told her, Coop,'' he chided. ''You should have told her just who you are, and about the special run. Hell, she thinks this is a regular trip, Coop, not some frolic for the local lawmakers before we have to return to our tame, sedate lives down in Tucson as ordinary ranchers and merchants. Hell, Coop, you've got to tell her.''

Cooper shook his head. ''No,'' he grinned. ''Not yet.'' He was silent again, his mind working. ''And I want you to tell the others not to say anything to Miss O'Rourke about who I am and what my real name is.'' The smile had reached his eyes, the amber flecks dancing. ''Can you see Jonathan?'' he laughed. ''Can you picture the look on his face when he meets his new employee? His brand-new efficiency expert!?''

Estevan shook his head. ''I presume he doesn't know that he's hired a woman,'' he breathed.

Cooper nodded. ''You know Jonathan and what he thinks about women, about where they belong. . . .''

It was an old litany, one they had joked about when they were boys. The memory of Jonathan's pronouncements—if not the sentiment—again evoked shared laughter. '' 'Only three places a woman's any good,' '' Estevan began, the timbre of his voice changing as he delivered an uncanny parody of Jonathan's officious incantations. " 'In a man's bed, in his kitchen . . .' ' '

" '. . . or dancing bare-assed naked on top of a bawdy house bar!' " Cooper finished, unable to contain himself. The laughter roared from deep within. Finally he managed to stop and control himself. Placing two fingers in his mouth, he put forth a loud, earsplitting whistle. The young man who handled the livestock responded to his call. "I want the team hitched now, Benjy; right now!" he bellowed. The hostler held up four fingers, but Dundee shook his head. "The full six! I'm going to give the lady a real ride!"

Jonathan Dundee stared angrily out of the window at the Phoenix office of Dundee Transport. "Sorry, that's all there was, Mr. Dundee," the young telegrapher reiterated, inwardly cringing at the scowl on the older man's face.

Jonathan discharged the clerk with a single wave of his hand as he looked at the sheet of yellow paper in front of him and again read aloud. "Left late," he breathed, his jaws tightening. Inwardly, he fumed. *Damn you, Coop. Goddamn you!*

He hated the waiting, and the sense of helplessness that came with it. It was bad enough not knowing exactly what time his half brother had seen fit to leave Prescott, without the added aggravation of knowing that when he did leave, he was behind schedule.

The large clock on the far wall added to the man's growing consternation, for it was as if the timepiece was mocking him. The heavy brass pendulum dragged against the walnut case, and slowly, imperceivably, the ornate minute hand crawled across the painted face, finally completing another full mark as one more minute disappeared into the past.

Jonathan spun around in his chair, facing the window. At thirty-six, he was a big man, broad shouldered and barrel chested, an imposing figure dressed in the fashion and style befitting his wealth and position. The summer-weight corduroy suit of pale brown was topped by a patterned ivory vest that was carefully tailored to complement his large frame, the color fitting his fair skin. Sandy eyebrows and a carefully trimmed beard enhanced his well-set blue eyes. He was, in appearance and outward temperament, a fitting heir to the Dundee name—a thrifty and shrewd young Scots lawyer with lairdly ways and a promising future.

Jonathan turned back to his desk and looked at the telegram. All this discord, this constant bickering, was finally going to stop. When O'Rourke arrived from the East, when Cooper and his mother—Jonathan's stepmother—saw it all spelled out in black and white and heard it from a man trained to assess and evaluate such matters, it would all stop. And his half brother would no longer be the proverbial thorn in Jonathan's side, a continual source of embarrassment, for then Jonathan would finally be able to sell. He crumpled up the telegram, holding it for a time in his clenched fist, and then tossed it into the wastebasket.

Chapter 2

Coop prided himself on just how well he had kept his word. He was giving the lady a ride, all right: a full span of six well-broken horses at a full run, over terrain guaranteed to make a grown man beg for mercy. He tore across the countryside, raising a dense cloud of dust and grit that covered man and beast with a thick coat of white grime.

It was, he well knew, hell for those inside the coach—the legislators and that woman and her child. The leather window curtains did little to protect the interior from the infiltration of dust and debris, and they turned the air hot and stagnant besides.

Estevan was up on top with Cooper, hanging on for dear life, the fingers of one hand desperately knotted around the thin siderail, the fingernails of his other hand imbedded in the horsehide seat. Twice he called out to Cooper, pleading with him to slow down, and felt the words ripped from his mouth by the wind. Finally he gave up trying to communicate his fears and instead concentrated on prayer.

He was starting his third Hail Mary, his eyes turned toward the heavens, when he discovered that She wasn't listening any better than Cooper. His eyes widened, and he stared up the side of the mountain; then he turned his gaze back to the road. They were approaching a curve, a great outcropping of rock and juniper obscuring the path that lay beyond the bend.

Estevan's eyes swept up the side of the canyon again, and he cursed silently at what he saw.

The side of the hill was thick with pine and scrub oak, the vegetation dense almost to the top. Huge boulders dotted the hillock, poking out from the bright green with a deceiving look of permanence. But something was wrong, ominously wrong.

Estevan saw the fresh scarring, a wide chasm torn through the lush growth. The upturned earth cut a vivid, irregular gash down the side of the mountain, a jumble of uprooted trees and shrubs marking the path of a rockslide. *A recent rockslide*. His eyes measured the track of the slide, and he fixed the direction, rapidly calculating the distance and the intensity of the fall. *"Coop!"* He shouted the man's name, swallowing the word and a mouth full of grit. None too gently, he gave the man a quick poke with his elbow.

Cooper turned his head. He saw the worry in Estevan's eyes and followed his friend's gaze toward the side of the mountain. His mouth dropped open, his lips forming a plaintive cry Estevan could not hear. *Oh, my God . . .*

He pulled back on the reins, taking up slack and winding the leather around his forearms as he braced his feet against the bottom of the box. He could feel the lead horses responding to his sudden commands, the lines vibrating as the animals tucked in their heads to escape the increased pressure of their bits. There was a sudden yawing to the left, the coach teetering on two wheels as they made the turn, unseating the passengers.

Cooper continued his seesaw battle with the team, pulling back on the reins in an effort to slow them down, and knew the very real fear of a sudden shift in weight. The coach swayed away from the cliff, taking the turn on the two outside wheels, sliding closer to the outer edge of the road. A ridge of gravel at the shoulder mounded and then tumbled over the side of the cliff following the path of an earlier slide. Out of the corner of his eyes, Cooper could see the rock showering into the yawning chasm that stretched far below him, and he immediately thought of his father and the way he had died. He closed his eyes against the memory and was jarred into awareness by another poke in the ribs.

They made the turn, swerving a second time to avoid the thick scattering of rocks and boulders strewn across the roadway. The two-wheeled ride continued for another fifty feet, and then, miraculously, the coach righted itself. The big Concord bounced deeply on the leather thoroughbraces, adding to the misery of those within and without. It seemed forever before the normal pitch and sway resumed, and even longer before the team finally came to a halt.

Cooper scrambled down from the box. He opened the leeward door and, unable to restrain himself, began to laugh.

Regan O'Rourke picked herself up from the bottom of the coach. Her dress was hiked to her knees, displaying the attractively molded calves of her long, long legs. She was aware of Cooper's gaze and struggled to hold her temper. It was a losing battle. Her eyes gave the first indication of the magnitude of her anger. They grew large, the irises suddenly luminous and the color of blue ice.

"You incompetent fool," she began as she clambered outside to confront him. She half turned to face the pile of rock, her outstretched arm pointing at the road and then moving up the face of the cliff. "How could you miss seeing this?" she asked, not really wanting an answer and not feeling that he was capable of giving a reasonable one. The sarcasm was even worse when she turned back to face him. "Going a bit too fast, perhaps? Too busy . . ." her eyebrow raised and she canted her head, ". . . entertaining your friend?"

Estevan retreated at her last remark, leaving Cooper to face the woman alone. She continued her appraisal, her eyes on the team. "You've got some injured livestock, Mr. Cooper. I suggest you try and concentrate on your job and see what can be done to help them." The dismissal was curt, swift—as effective as if a door had slammed between them.

Cooper stood for a time, his cheeks crimson. He rubbed his chin, considering the attractive possibility of throwing the woman over a cliff before concluding there were too damn many witnesses.

His mood changed, and he shaded his eyes, staring up the side of the hill. He searched the rim, not sure what he was looking for, taking his time as he marked the path of the rocky avalanche. It was the wrong time of the year, he thought to himself. His eyes swept the rough terrain for a long way north and south, lifting to examine the cloudless sky. No rain and sure as hell no snow. No reason for the slide.

Cooper felt the woman's eyes on his back and bunched his shoulders in an attempt to escape her scrutiny. He did not succeed. "I know," he said, surrendering, "I know. . . ." Without turning around, he headed for the team.

It was as if someone had opened the very gates of hell. The wind pushed the heat before it, rolling the air across the yellow desert in great shimmering waves that distorted the landscape and drove the sand creatures into hiding beneath the rocks.

There was no shade. The sun hung directly overhead, pinpointing the cacti and scrub and stealing their shadows. Small black circles at the base of each plant sheltered only the most minute animal life, and then only from the light.

Regan O'Rourke paced up and down beside the coach, fighting the stiffness in her long legs. She had attended to all the personal tasks that could modestly be attended to under the circumstances and had stood patiently by as Michael did the same. As Michael ran up to her now, she sighed and asked herself if despite the inconvenience she should have left Michael back at the army fort and picked him up after her job for Dundee Transport was completed. There were people there who would have cared for him—people who had known her brother and his wife. But after she had seen Michael, she could not bear to leave him. He had seemed so small, so vulnerable in the big white bed at the fort infirmary. No, she could never have left him behind.

"He's going to fix everything, Regan. Coop says he's going to fix everything just fine!"

The boy's enthusiastic declaration roused the woman from her dark musings. She dabbed at her forehead with her handkerchief, reaching out quickly to catch the child before he dashed away again. "And did your Mr. Cooper also tell you how long it will be before he's done?"

Michael was dancing back and forth at the end of some unseen tether. His head bobbed up and down beneath the battered felt Stetson he had refused to surrender, but he didn't answer. At least, not out loud. The woman tried again. "When, Michael? Did Mr. Cooper tell you when we will be on our way again?"

The youngster recognized the no-nonsense tone in his aunt's voice. "Soon," he said, eager to be away. "Real soon." He twisted free of the woman's grasp and was gone, racing past the four legislators who were looking in vain for some shade in which to sit.

Cooper Dundee was on one knee beside the lead horse, cursing his ill luck. Gingerly, he worked his hand up and down the animal's foreleg, his sensitive fingers aware of the subtle differences in the temperature of the gelding's flesh. The swelling had already begun, the bay's hide quivering in response to the man's probing fingers, the involuntary twitch rising in waves from cocked hoof to shoulder. Disgusted, Cooper swore. "Damn! Goddamn!"

Estevan Folley was beside him, squatting down, his right hand absently stroking the big gelding's chest. "How bad, Coop?" There was a degree of censure in the man's voice that he was unable to conceal.

"Bad enough." Cooper met Estevan's gaze, his eyes narrowing. "Don't say it, *compadre*," he breathed. "Just don't say it." He'd heard all he wanted from the woman—and then some.

Estevan ignored the entreaty. The acrimonious relationship between Cooper and the O'Rourke woman had worsened with every mile. Cooper's stubborn refusal to consider what had happened a preventable accident had made matters even worse. "There's a valid side to her argument, Coop." Estevan's tone was that of a priest in a confessional. "You've been pushing the horses ever since we left the way station. Ever since we left Prescott."

"I won't be needing your help for a few minutes, Estevan." It was as if Cooper had not heard one word that his friend had said; worse, he had chosen to ignore him. Shaking his head, Estevan accepted his friend's subtle dismissal and headed back to the coach.

Michael trotted over to Cooper. He was everywhere at once, mimicking Cooper's every move, seemingly unaffected by the intense heat. "Is it broke, Coop?" He ran his small fingers up and down the bay's leg, plopping down into the dirt when the animal lifted the injured limb and knocked him off balance. Unabashed, he scrambled back to his feet. "You going to shoot him, Coop?" The boy's concern was sudden and real.

The stage driver shook his head and lifted the boy out of the way. "He's going to be fine, Michael." He winked at the boy and pulled the hat down over his eyes. "He's going to be just fine." Standing up, he hoisted Michael onto his shoulder and headed back toward the coach.

The woman was back inside. The interior of the old carriage was the only place where she had found any respite from the hot sun. "Well?" Regan demanded.

Cooper forced a smile and boosted Michael through the window. He waited until the boy was settled in his seat and then answered the woman's question. "I'm going to have to unhitch the lead horse and its mate," he began. Half turning, he gestured toward the team, feeling a need to escape her eyes.

She nodded. "And how long will that take?"

Cooper faced her and involuntarily flinched when he saw her fondling her watch pendant. He bit his tongue against the angry words that threatened to tumble from his mouth: *From when I start until I finish.* Out loud, he said, "With some help from Estevan, ten, maybe twenty minutes." He answered the next question before she was able to ask it. "I'll tie them behind. It's going to mean making the rest of the trip at a near walk, but it's the best I can do."

Her eyes widened. "The best you *could* have done, Mr. Cooper, was to use a bit more discretion as to speed, and a little less dime-novel bravado." She answered his smile with one that mirrored the same lack of sincerity.

It was all Cooper could do to keep from strangling her. He shut his eyes, intent on driving the thought away, and found himself reveling in visions of the woman staked out on an anthill. "All right," he conceded. He resented the way she had berated him for his carelessness, implying that he had purposely abused the team. "I take care of the livestock, Miss O'Rourke. I don't do anything intentionally that puts my animals in any kind of danger." When she started to speak, he silenced her, his gloved fingers pressed against her lips. She pushed his hand away but said nothing, glaring at him furiously. He continued, "I can't see through solid rock. I had no idea when we came around that bend that we'd run into this kind of trouble. Not now. Not this time of year. It's not usual to have rockslides without rain. It was an *accident*, Miss O'Rourke. And there isn't a driver on this line that could have foreseen it. Not one."

Regan stared directly into the man's eyes as she breathed, "Two thousand miles. In the last six months, I've traveled over two thousand miles. By train. By ferry. By coach. And in all those miles, not one accident, Mr. Cooper. Not one incident of driver incompetence."

There was a slight shifting—a swaying—as Aaron Beitermann and the other legislators climbed back into the coach on the other side. The four men were painfully aware of the strain between the driver and the woman, just as they were conscious of their words. They pretended not to notice, determined to make the best of an uncomfortable situation. When Beitermann produced a flask of brandy, the others were eminently grateful.

Regan didn't care if the others heard her or not. "I think it's time you tended the horses and made some effort to get on with it. *Now,* Mr. Cooper," she finished.

Cooper said nothing. He stood there for a time, his jaws working, and then turned away.

Beitermann cleared his throat, sorry that he had held his tongue so long. *Women,* he mused to himself. *Give them a little responsibility, and it goes right to their head.* He fortified himself with a swig from his bottle. *Next thing you know, they'll be wanting the vote, and then—God forbid! —the right to hold office.* . . . He leaned forward, intending to chastise the woman, but was cut short by the boy.

"You shouldn't holler at him, Regan." Michael's face bore the petulant pout of a child who had been abruptly separated from a favorite playmate who didn't meet with his parents' approval. He refused to look at his aunt, choosing instead to lean out the window and follow Cooper with his eyes. "You shouldn't holler at him. . . ."

Regan reached out to the child, her hand hovering at his shoulder. She heard Beitermann's whispered "amen" and the murmured agreement of the others, and felt totally alone. They didn't understand. They didn't even try to understand. She had a job to do, and she was doing it. The very best she knew how.

The tick of the clock was the loudest sound to be heard in Jonathan Dundee's Phoenix office. The two men had reached an impasse, their mutual silence as intense as the words that had passed between them only moments before.

Cooper took another long drink from the crystal decanter he had taken from his brother's desk. The potent scotch burned his throat and made his voice whiskey hoarse. "Anyway," he said, "we ended up with two lame horses and some bumps and bruises inside. Nothing serious. Beitermann lost his brandy, and Les Moorhouse lost his lunch—but no one was really hurt."

His speech ended, he raked his fingers through his hair and was aware of a dull ache in his shoulders. He flexed them, looking at his brother, and saw from the man's face that he was going to have to say more. "I wasn't drinking, Jonathan," he began. The bottle that he held in his hand seemed to refute his statement, and he put it down. "I don't drink on the job." His words had become defensive. "Not anymore."

"Sure." Jonathan's tone betrayed his doubts. He was remembering the way things had been, the way Coop acted after Malachai died: ranting like a wild man—even before the funeral—that Malachai had been murdered, that it had not been an accident. Just like he claimed the rockslide wasn't an accident.

And the drinking . . . For almost six months Cooper had buried himself in the bordellos and the bars, growing more silent and drinking himself into a perpetual stupor—on the job and off.

Jonathan shook a finger at Cooper as if he were talking to a recalcitrant child. "This is a business! Not some toy that Malachai created for his own amusement—or for *your* amusement! You were wrong to make this trip." He was still shaking his finger. "It's totally impractical, far too costly!"

"Bull!" Cooper's answer came from deep within his burning gut. He took another drink, hoping to quench the fire. "I'm finishing the run, Jonathan."

Nose to nose, the physical contrast between the half brothers was striking. It was more than the distinct difference in coloring and bearing, or in their attire. Of the two, Jonathan was the more imposing. Six foot five in his leather-heeled boots, he towered above his younger brother, his massive frame seeming to dwarf the other. Aware of the way the difference in height had always intimidated Cooper, he pulled himself even more erect. "No, you're not finishing the run, Coop."

Cooper shrugged, ignoring his brother's firm refusal. "I'll haul the mail and the payroll from Fort McDowell to Tucson on schedule and still make the special run." He faced his brother and saw the argument forming behind the blue eyes. *Now,* he thought. *I'll tell him now.* "Regan O'Rourke's here." He chose his next words carefully. "Showed up at the office in Prescott and insisted on making the ride in with the rest of us." The ploy worked.

"O'Rourke!" Jonathan was visibly pleased. His anticipation at the arrival of the efficiency expert he had hired from the East overshadowed his anger of only moments before. "Where is he?"

Cooper managed to control his smile. "Out there," he said, nodding toward the door that separated Jonathan's office from the outer waiting room. "Right out there." He didn't want another drink but took one anyway, needing something to drown the sudden urge to laugh.

He watched as Jonathan pulled back the edge of the green shade that covered the door's multipaned window. There was a long silence as the man explored the full length of the waiting room. Finally, waggling a finger at Cooper, Jonathan beckoned his brother to him. "Where?" he whispered.

"Right there." Coop smiled as he tapped the window with the tip of his finger, ducking away when the woman responded and stared directly at the glass. Just as quickly she glanced away, quieting the young boy who squirmed and fidgeted in the seat beside her.

Jonathan's face was a study in shades of purple. His fingers still arched against the canvas shade, he stood as if frozen in place. The skin at his collar mottled and turned an even deeper red. "A woman," he sputtered. He turned his head, facing his brother, hoping it was a joke, some perverse prank. "Very funny, Cooper. Now, where's *Mr*. O'Rourke?" *That had to be it; she is the man's wife*. . . . He took another covert look through the glass, measuring the woman with a practiced eye.

The younger Dundee took his time answering, enjoying the taste of Jonathan's imported liquor—and Jonathan's obvious consternation. Satisfied that his brother had suffered enough, he crossed to the door. There was another moment of hesitation as he waited for Jonathan to withdraw slightly, and then he pulled open the door. "Miss O'Rourke," he greeted. The exaggerated bow came as an afterthought, and he was smiling when he straightened to face her. "Miss O'Rourke," he stood back, opening the door wide, "Mr. Dundee; Mr. Jonathan Dundee."

The office seemed to shrink. Jonathan retreated to the place behind his desk, his eyes flashing strong telepathic messages to Cooper that conveyed more than any spoken word. Cooper answered with a smile as he backed against the far wall. He stood there, arms crossed, content to watch.

"Mr. Dundee." Regan moved across the floor with a firm step, her hand extended.

There was a long silence, an awkward pause as Jonathan collected his wits. He reached out, taking the woman's hand, surprised at the unladylike response in her strong fingers, the almost masculine manner with which she returned his silent greeting. "Miss O'Rourke," he said finally. He cleared his throat and began again. "I'm afraid, Miss O'Rourke, that there has been an unfortunate misunderstanding—" he paused, nodding at Cooper "—and that my brother has contributed to that misunderstanding. You see, I don't employ women, Miss O'Rourke." He shifted his gaze to his brother. "Dundee Transport doesn't employ women."

Regan inhaled sharply, the sound of her sudden breath

cutting into the silence that had again descended on the room. Her eyes swung from one man to the other. "Your brother . . . ?" She realized, then, what was happening. She was an unwary pawn in a game of cat and mouse, the butt of a sibling joke. Cooper Dundee had played her for the fool, and Jonathan Dundee was about to do the same.

Smiling, she met Jonathan's gaze fully, refusing to yield to his eyes and determined not to yield to her own temper. "I have a contract, Mr. Dundee. *We* have a contract. . . ." Without lowering her eyes, she began to dig through her bag. The pressboard envelope appeared between her fingers, and she held it before her with an air of authority. "An agreement," she began, quoting almost verbatim, "between one Jonathan Dundee and the firm of O'Rourke and Associates, for services rendered for a period of not less than one month or more than three. An agreement that you—as senior partner in this firm—signed and had properly witnessed."

The smile failed to reach her eyes, and lessened when she heard Cooper's whispered "Damn!" as he delighted in their joint discomfort.

"Unless, Mr. Dundee, you are suggesting that your younger brother forged your signature. In which case, he would not only be guilty of forgery, but also guilty of *fraud*!" She purposely emphasized the word, clearly conveying the message to Cooper that she had no intention of forgetting his deception. The envelope was still in her hand, and she tapped it solidly against Jonathan's broad chest, one tap for each word. "You will honor this contract, Mr. Dundee. I'm going to insist that you honor this contract."

Jonathan backed away from the woman, momentarily surprised by her brazen attack. He recovered, but his ire was fueled by Cooper's silent role as the amused observer. "You never told me you were a woman," he raged. He brushed aside the woman's hand, his index finger thumping against her bodice as he took the offensive. "In all your letters, including your initial response to my inquiries, you never once said that you were a woman!''

Regan's fingers closed around the man's wrist, and she pushed his hand away. This time the smile fired her eyes and brought color to her cheeks. ''Well, Mr. Dundee, you never once asked!''

Jonathan was shaking his head. His lawyer's pride refused to admit defeat, and his masculine pride fogged his thinking. ''I won't have a woman working for me. Not now. Not ever. You're fired, Miss O'Rourke.''

She laughed, totally unaffected by the man's attempt to dismiss her. ''And you, Mr. Dundee, are a pompous ass!'' Her voice changed, the words coming with a crisp air of authority. ''You have until tomorrow morning, Mr. Dundee, to agree to honor the contract as it stands, or to forfeit a substantial amount of cash for work already done.'' She saw the look on his face and produced her notebook. ''My initial report of your operations, Mr. Dundee, as it relates to the route between Prescott and this office.'' He started to reply, but she stopped him, shaking her head. ''Tomorrow, Mr. Dundee. We'll talk again tomorrow. I'll be in the hotel across the street.''

Turning on her heel, she swept past Cooper without one backward look, pausing only long enough to pull Michael to his feet and hurry him through the outer door. There was something very final in the way she slammed the door, rattling the windows in their frames. The whole building seemed to shudder in the wake of her retreat.

Cooper pushed himself away from the wall, staring into the near darkness in the front office. ''And what now, big brother?'' As he awaited his brother's reply, he realized just how much he enjoyed these sparring matches with Jonathan—particularly when he had the upper hand.

Jonathan cursed, vehemently. ''Why the hell didn't you at least give me some warning before bringing her in here?'' He stopped, throwing up his hands in utter disgust when he realized what a fool he had been. "It took me six months to find someone willing to make this kind of an evaluation." He hated it, the feeling that he needed the woman for her expertise. "I guess I can't fire her after all, dammit." Then, laying the blame for the bulk of the difficulty at his brother's feet, he declared, "*You're* going to have to convince her to continue."

Cooper shook his head, his grin spreading. He'd had all he could take of that woman in Prescott, and twice as much when they were making the run. It was his brother's turn now. "*Your* contract, Jonathan." He headed for the door, savoring this latest victory . . . which was far more potent than Jonathan's imported scotch. "*Your* problem." And then he was gone.

Chapter 3

The hotel dining room was filled with the usual collection of solitary transients, a single guest at each table. The only noise was the sound of their eating and the even cadence of their forks against the brown stoneware.

Seated with Michael, Regan O'Rourke toyed with her dinner, her stomach rumbling in protest to the worries that continued to assault her mind. There was Michael to consider now and the responsibilities she faced in providing him with a home. In the end, it always came down to the need of money.

"I'd like more milk, Regan." Michael's voice penetrated the woman's thoughts. "Please?"

She reached out, touching the boy's cheek, grateful that with Cooper no longer a visible rival, she and the boy had effected a truce. "I thought little boys had to be coaxed to drink milk," she said softly. Immediately she regretted the words. The pout had returned, and she felt the boy pull away from her touch.

"I'm not a baby, Regan."

"Michael . . ." Her hand hovered at the boy's shoulder. She hated it when he withdrew, when the corners of his small mouth turned down in an expression of censure that was so damned familiar. She averted her eyes, staring into her plate. "I'm sorry, Michael. I . . ."

"Miss O'Rourke?" Jonathan Dundee stood beside their

table, hat in hand. He waited, hoping that she would make the initial move, and when she did not, he nodded toward the extra chair. "I'd like to talk, Miss O'Rourke."

Carefully, Regan explored the man's face. "No flowers, Mr. Dundee? No box of candy?"

He returned her smile, cautiously, appraising the woman with a fresh eye. "Would that have worked?"

She laughed, and it was a pleasant sound. "It never has." Her hand closed around the back of the empty chair, and she pulled it out from the table. "Business, Mr. Dundee. For the next—" she tilted her head to look at her watch "—thirty-five minutes, I am free to discuss business."

Jonathan sat. "And the boy?" He reached out, ruffling the youngster's hair without looking at him. "Is he your advisor?"

"My nephew, Mr. Dundee. Michael Patrick O'Rourke." She tapped the boy's elbow and urged him to rise, at the same time signaling for the waitress.

Jonathan reached out again to shake the boy's hand, stopping himself when the boy ignored him. He withdrew his hand, grateful when the young serving girl returned to the table with a fresh pot of coffee and a clean cup and saucer.

Regan conferred with the young woman for a brief moment and then turned her attention back to the boy. "Michael, it's getting late. I want you to go up to our room and go to sleep. Hannah"—she indicated the waitress with a single nod—"will stay with you until Mr. Dundee and I are through." There was a brief silence as she waited for the boy to do as he was told.

When Michael was gone, she answered Jonathan's unspoken question, as if she could read his mind. "Michael was the reason for my unexpected arrival in Prescott," she began. "My brother . . ." She swallowed against the dull ache at the back of her throat. "My brother was serving at Fort Whipple when the cholera epidemic broke out among the Indian scouts. Before it was over, Brian and his wife and their baby were dead. Michael was left. . . ." Her voice broke, and then faded. It took her a moment to regain her composure, but when she did, the inner pain was all that remained. "Now, Mr. Dundee, you said that you wanted to discuss business."

Jonathan stared at the woman in unabashed amazement. There were no tears, no visible indications that she was in great emotional distress. She was, the man noted, in total control of her emotions.

And, he thought, *absolutely stunning.*

After finishing their coffee, Regan and Jonathan decided to continue their discussion in the sitting room of Regan's small suite. There they lingered over a final brandy, neither one wanting to end what had become—surprisingly—a pleasant conclusion to an otherwise unpleasant day.

Jonathan spoke in a hushed voice, aware of the small boy sleeping in the next room. "I'd like you to make the rest of the run, Regan—the special run. It does take longer than usual, though, because the stagecoach stops at Casa Grande and the Dundee homestead before going on to Tucson."

She nodded, one eyebrow raising as she considered his words. "And your brother will be driving." It was more a wary statement of fact than a question.

"My half brother," he said. Somehow, the words sounded harsher than he intended, and he felt the familiar embarrassment that always preceded the mandatory explanations of Cooper's existence. "You'll meet his mother, Teresa, at the way station just south of Casa Grande," he said softly. "The home ranch." There was a long silence as he considered his next words.

Regan's response to the man's sudden quiet was tender and compassionate. She reached out, her hand lingering on his sleeve. "You don't have to talk about it, Jonathan. If it causes you pain, there's no need to discuss any of it."

He was grateful for her concern, and even more grateful that she didn't exhibit the usual womanly curiosity about his

father's second wife. "I certainly can't blame Coop," he
began. "I don't even blame Malachai. . . . You see, Teresa
was a servant there, supposedly taking care of my mother,
and instead she made herself . . . available to my father." He
shook his head. "My mother killed herself because of Teresa,"
he said bitterly. He finished the remainder of his brandy in
one long swallow, then faced the woman. He held up the
empty glass. "Lubrication for an otherwise silent tongue,"
he smiled. "I should have known better, and I hope that
you'll forgive me."

It was, Regan thought, an eloquent apology. "There's
nothing to forgive, Jonathan. Sometimes . . ." She caught
herself, her eyes on the door to the bedroom. She could hear
Michael's soft breathing and wondered if he was really asleep.
Secrets, she thought. *We live in a world filled with so many
painful secrets.* . . .

"Regan?" Seeing the sadness in her face, Jonathan called
her name softly, his eyes filled with concern.

She smiled up at him. "It's nothing," she lied. "I was just
thinking of Michael."

He kissed her. It seemed the natural thing to do, and he
was pleased when she didn't resist. He was just as pleased
when she pulled away and asked him to leave.

He left the room, whistling. He'd found a decent woman; a
decent woman with beauty and brains.

Regan undressed in the dark, concerned that she might
disturb Michael and rouse him from an untroubled sleep. As
careful as she was, every sound still seemed magnified ten
times over, and she bit her lower lip at the crisp rustle of the
starched sheets as she slipped into the large double bed next
to the boy. She lay there on her back, not daring to move.

"I don't like him." Michael's voice sounded harsh and
strained against the darkness. He rolled over until he, too,
was lying on his back. "I don't like him."

Regan sighed. She reached for the boy's hand and held him fast. "He's a good man, Michael."

There was a sound as the boy shook his head back and forth on his pillow. He was remembering the snatches of conversation he had heard when his aunt and the man were talking. "He said—" The boy forced himself to remember just the right words. "He said that Coop was . . ." He stumbled over the word, forgetting a syllable. "Ir-sponsible, and that he didn't know anything about running a stage line."

So that was it. It wasn't Jonathan himself; it was Jonathan's truths about his brother. Regan felt the boy try to pull away from her, and she wound her fingers more tightly around his small fist. "Jonathan is very much like your father, Michael," she said softly. *Like the man you remember as your father,* she thought.

"No!" The boy's answer came from deep within him, so deep that the bed shook with the force of his words. "No!" He struggled to get his hand free and turned over on his side, his back to the woman as he curled into a tight ball. "Coop's like Pa," he sniffed. "Coop."

Regan knew that the boy was crying. She put her arm around him and pulled him close to her stomach, feeling the warmth of his tears on her arm. This time he didn't pull away from her touch, but neither did he really respond. "Coop," he whispered, and then he was quiet for a brief moment. "Coop's like my pa," he breathed, and drifted off to sleep.

From the mouths of babes, Regan thought ruefully. She closed her eyes, still holding on to the child, trying to conjure up the image of Jonathan's face. Only it wasn't Jonathan she saw. It was Cooper. Cooper Dundee, with the mocking green eyes and a smile that was filled with teasing and promises.

Cooper's face hovered before her—and the face of someone else. Someone so much the same. Someone from long ago.

The pain came then, the pain in her head and the deeper one inside her breast. The pain of having loved well but not

wisely. She pulled Michael closer and promised herself she
would never feel that pain again.

Cooper Dundee and Estevan Folley staggered out the back
door of the bordello, sated and drunk—very, very drunk.
Stumbling along the dark alleyway, Cooper reached out and
grabbed Estevan's arm for support and then pulled him to a
shaky standstill. Backs against the wall, they stood thère,
sharing a bottle and silently reflecting on their troubles.

Estevan took a final pull on the bottle. He lifted a numb
foot and spent a long moment raking at the air in search of
the ground. Giving up, he slid unceremoniously down the
side of the building and collided with the ground. Cooper
followed him. Side by side, they passed the bottle back and
forth, neither one wanting the rotgut, but each of them unwill-
ing to be the first to admit he'd had more than enough.

Cooper shook his head, the faint breeze carrying the whine
of something far away. Snatches of a reedy melody came to
him, and he pounded his ear with an open palm, thinking the
music was coming from inside his head. But the noise did not
stop. It rose, fell, and came again, bits and pieces of a
melody that reached out to him. "Amazing Grace," he
breathed.

Estevan stirred. He opened one eye and stared at what he
hoped was Cooper's head. "Amazing Grace," he echoed. He
brightened. "I remember her!" he exclaimed. "She's the one
at Rosa's Cantina with the big . . ." He held his hands in
front of his chest, cupped palms upturned as if he were
juggling two ripe melons.

Cooper took a swipe at him with both hands, boxing his
ears. "No, you damned fool! That was *Mama Teta Grande*!
'Amazing Grace' is a song—a song they play when people
die." He canted his head, straining to hear.

Estevan dropped his bottle. "Are we dead, Cooper?" He
patted his stomach, knowing that if he wasn't already dead,
by morning he'd be wishing he was.

Cooper didn't answer. He was trying to get up. He fell, righted himself, and then fell again. Finally, he made it, pulling Estevan upright with him. Still hanging onto the man's sleeve, he began following the sound of the organ, the tune guiding their steps.

They came into the street, their pathway illuminated by the flickering yellow glow of a double row of lanterns ahead. A canvas tent stood at the end of the string of lights, the flap open. Inside, a middle-aged woman sat at a small pump organ, her fingers gliding over the keys as she played the hymn, her sweet voice a whisper above the flutelike tones. "Amazing Grace, how sweet the sound, that saved a wretch like me. . . ."

There was the press of a small crowd at Cooper's back, and he felt himself being pushed and jostled forward. He tried to turn and found himself face to face with a large family marching three abreast. They kept coming, pushing a reluctant Estevan before them.

It was as if the hand of God were pushing them, and there was no escape. Taking it as a sign—and feeling suddenly reverent and in need of repentance—the two men gave up. Meekly, they took their seats in the front row.

The evangelist was dressed in black, the severe cut of his Prince Albert coat making him look tall and gaunt. Dark eyes flamed out from beneath bushy eyebrows, the fire of salvation and torment increasing the man's hungry look of privation. He moved constantly, pacing the length of the plank stage with the heavy stride of a man with a great mission. Up and down he marched, his hands clenched behind his back, his mouth moving noiselessly as he prayed to his God for guidance.

Suddenly he whirled, facing the crowd and pointing a long skeletal finger at the two nearest transgressors. "Brethren," he shouted, "ye have sinned!"

The words roared out into the tent, reverberating with a force that belied the man's consumptive appearance. So intense was their power, that Cooper was knocked from his seat. Still drunk, he tumbled over backward, unable to catch himself, and became an instant convert.

It was a glorious sermon. Cooper and Estevan sat as if mesmerized, their fingers tightly wrapped around the edge of the narrow bench.

Up and down the evangelist strode, pausing now and then to thrust a finger at some unwary soul deserving of his immediate attention. An old man snoring in the back row; a gossipy woman in the middle; the fretful child in the front. No one escaped his watchful eye. For almost an hour he preached his hellfire and damnation religion, exhorting those who had sinned to come forward, to take the first step toward eternal salvation.

The response was slow in coming, and only a trickle of weary sinners made their way to the podium. He blessed them, the old and infirm who were worried about dying, and sent them back to their seats.

"Don't think, brothers and sisters, that God will not have you. Don't think, children, that you have sinned and cannot be forgiven! God forgives everybody," he exclaimed solemnly. "Yes, brothers, even me! Even a man who once succumbed to all the pleasures of the flesh." He rose up on his tiptoes, thumping his chest. "A liar and a cheat!" He took off his tie and opened the top buttons of his shirt. "A drunkard! A whoremonger who sold his own sisters into bondage!"

There was an audible gasp from the crowd, and a chorus of fervent "Amen, amen . . .''

"Not the sisters of my flesh or bone of my bone," he cried. "But my sisters—as we are all brothers and sisters— who were the daughters of Adam!" The old man choked back a tear. "I am ashamed of my sin, my children, just as I am ashamed of the sinful lives of those I led astray.

"Must I suffer forever?" he cried. "Must I forever bear the guilt for those women whom I led into iniquity, but who refused to follow me into the light? Evil women," he breathed, leaning forward, his voice hoarse. "Women who loved the wickedness of the flesh more than the purity of redemption. Did they care what pain they brought?'' The preacher beckoned for an answer with both hands.

''No!'' came the reply.

''Did they care that Satan paid them court and diseased their flesh?'' Again he prompted a negative reply, more women than men responding. ''Did they care that they destroyed the homes of other women, or stole their men?''

There was another resounding ''No!'' and a murmured echo as wives and sweethearts prodded their mates with their elbows.

''Shame on these women,'' the old man intoned, shaking his finger, ''lying there on their unholy beds, shameless in their nakedness.'' A new fire sparked the old man's eyes. ''Writhing in pleasure as they toy with their own bodies and taunt and tease those men who dare to approach them. Picture them, my children. See them as they fling open their legs like the very gates of hell, bidding the fools to enter. . . .''

Cooper was on his feet. ''Amen!'' he shouted, seeing in his mind's eye the very women the old man was describing. There was a surge of warmth, a pleasant dull ache in his groin as the picture became even more vivid. *''Hallelujah!''* he screamed.

He grabbed Estevan's arm and bolted down the aisle, dragging his friend with him. A dozen rowdies fell in behind.

Estevan had to run to keep up. ''Where are we going, Coop?'' he panted.

''Back to the bordello!'' came the answer. ''To assault the gates of hell!''

Chapter 4

There was a chill in the air, the damp earth surrendering its heat in waves of white vapor that left the harness leather feeling clammy and slick beneath Cooper's fingers. He swore, weaving the final knot and securing the last buckle. His fingers were numb, the tips heavy and leaden. His voice came out as a croak as he mumbled a terse good morning to the four legislators who climbed aboard the stagecoach one by one. Coop leaned against the coach, watching as his half brother approached carrying two steaming mugs in his hands.

"You manage to get any sleep?" Jonathan's tone was more genial than his words, and he cursed himself for not having made a greater effort.

Cooper was too hung over to be on the defensive, and yet there was a terseness in his words as well. "As much as I needed," he said finally.

Jonathan was determined to try again. He handed Cooper a mug of strong coffee, the brew generously laced with brandy from his office desk. "A little hair of the dog," he smiled. "A peace offering, Coop."

The younger man nodded. He closed his eyes, ignoring the searing pain against his tongue and throat as he took a long drink. The potent liquid rebounded in the pit of his empty stomach, and only his iron will kept it down. "Just what I needed," he lied.

They stood there for a time, the old awkwardness returning. The silences were worse now that they were aware of them, and it heightened their longing for their dead father. Malachai had been the glue that had bound them together, the gentle strength that muted the sharp differences that had become more obvious as they grew up and apart. They both started to speak at once, laughed at their collision of words, and were silent again.

Jonathan took the initiative, knowing that from habit— perhaps even respect—Cooper would hold his tongue. "Regan—Miss O'Rourke—is going to make the trip, Coop." He saw the look on his brother's face. "I made amends," he said truthfully. "She's going to continue her appraisal of the line." He was surprised when Cooper said nothing, simply nodding. "No objections?" he asked as he finished his mug of coffee.

Cooper poured the rest of his coffee on the ground, unable to drink it. "I saw her preliminary report. It was on your desk, so I took a look." He handed the empty cup to Jonathan. "The lady may be a hardhead," he said, thinking of her stubborn insistence that the accident at the rockslide was avoidable, "but she's an honest hardhead.

"She was one hundred percent right about the office in Prescott," Cooper went on. "The records are in a mess, and Cooney has a stack of complaints an inch thick over damaged freight and late deliveries. *His* late deliveries." He wanted Jonathan to understand that the line itself had adhered to its schedule, but that Cooney, the agent at the Prescott office, had failed to make his disbursements. "Will Michael be making the trip?" he suddenly asked, thinking of the boy.

Jonathan nodded. He had found himself separating the boy from Regan in his thoughts, as if the child didn't exist. "Regan"—this time he didn't bother to correct himself—"hired a woman here to take care of the boy at the hotel until she finishes touring the line." He shrugged. "The woman's changed her mind, and Regan doesn't have time to find anyone else to take her place. I told her to go ahead and take the boy; let him make the ride. It's not as if this is the regular run," he finished. "And the boy seems to be reasonably well behaved."

Cooper smiled in agreement. "He's a good kid, Jonathan. All boy and a yard wide!" His mood then changed, and he checked his watch. "The army's only got about ten minutes to get that dispatch they want delivered down to Tucson over here from Fort McDowell. If the messenger doesn't arrive, I'm leaving without him. I've got a schedule to maintain— especially in light of our appraiser."

Jonathan frowned. "The army expects you to make an exception, Coop. You knew that when we signed the contract."

Cooper shook his head. "*You* knew it. Major Anderson assumed it—and I set him straight. Our first responsibility is to the passengers who rely on us to make their connections. I told Anderson the last time he screwed up that I wasn't his glorified errand boy. I meant it." He held up his hand when Jonathan started to protest. "They managed to deliver the payroll on time," he said, nodding at the front boot, "and we've got a deadline for getting it to Tucson. And that takes precedence over Anderson and his brownnosing efficiency report to the adjutant at Fort Lowell." He tapped Jonathan's chest. "And you can tell him I said so."

"Coop . . ." Jonathan's reply was cut short by the arrival of Estevan Folley. Jonathan nodded his head in greeting, then retreated into the building.

Estevan's mood was grim. He had the look of impending death about him, his face haggard and a shade lighter than usual. "I hope you're satisfied, Coop." Each word felt as though it was preceded by a mouthful of feathers, and he scraped his thick tongue with his teeth. "In one night, you have destroyed the image that ten generations of Iberian nobility fought to preserve."

Estevan had come to the wrong place seeking sympathy. Cooper reached out, slapping the back of his hand against the man's tender belly. "You going to ride up top or inside with your venerable colleagues?"

The idea of riding anywhere brought spasms of pain and a bout of instant nausea. Still, there was the hope that if he did get sick, it would be all over Cooper. "On top," Estevan grinned. "Where else?"

Suspicious, Cooper eyed his friend through narrowed lids and was about to say something when Michael O'Rourke bounded up the sidewalk, followed closely by Regan. The boy was dressed more suitably than before, and Cooper's old Stetson was firmly pulled down over his ears.

"Good mornin', partner!" Cooper swept the boy off his feet and hoisted him up onto the driver's seat. "You're going to ride up top, Michael. You, me, and Estevan!" The boy let out a wild whoop as he proudly took his place.

Regan was less than delighted when Cooper lifted the boy to the top of the coach. She hurriedly moved forward to let her feelings be known but felt a tug at her elbow. "Let him be, Regan," Jonathan said, smiling down at her. Upon seeing her preparing to board the stage, Jonathan had rushed out of his office to greet her and was sorry that there were so many people already in the street.

She patted his hand. "I don't want him to get hurt, Jonathan."

The man shook his head, his eyes filled with the woman. She was wearing a plain, ivory-colored suit and a single piece of silver jewelry with sapphires that paled in the glow of her incredible, velvet-fringed blue eyes. "He'll be fine, Regan, just fine. Coop really likes the boy, and it's obvious that Michael feels the same."

Regan's smile was filled with a sweet irony. "I know. That's what worries me."

Feeling Cooper's eyes on them, Jonathan tilted his head and reached down to kiss Regan's cheek. From his seat, Cooper saw his brother's unusual show of affection, and as Jonathan helped Regan into the coach, Cooper leaned over to catch his eye. "You keep that up, Jonathan, and I'm going to be convinced that you've compromised her—" the pause was intentional "—neutrality."

The woman smiled her own curious smile. "I think not, Mr. Dundee. You see, unlike you, I know the difference between business and pleasure."

Estevan's laugh was almost a giggle. "Score one for the lady from the East," he murmured.

Cooper's two-word retort to Estevan tumbled up from his throat but froze in place on his tongue as he realized that Michael sat between them. "With any luck, *compadre,* your friend from last night has gifted you with a social disease," he crowed.

Michael turned, facing Estevan. "What's a social disease, Mr. Folley?"

The young legislator doubled over in laughter and waved the bewildered boy aside without a word.

Soon after the Dundee Transport Line stage left Phoenix for its next major stop, Casa Grande, halfway to Tucson, Logan Montgomery eased his considerable bulk into the chair in front of Jonathan's desk. The land speculator was a big man, soft in the way men grow soft when they hire others to do their work, but with a hardness in his eyes that betrayed his true nature. No matter what the expression on his face or the inflection in his voice, the eyes never changed.

He helped himself to a cigar, carefully trimming the ends with a gold clipper and conserving the refuse. These he crumpled between his fingers, toying with them as he spoke. "Why didn't you tell me O'Rourke was a woman?"

Jonathan smiled. "I didn't know, Logan," he answered truthfully. He shrugged. "It doesn't make any difference." Regan's handwritten report was on the desk before him, and he opened the folder and pushed it across the desk.

Montgomery picked up the missive. He read it, nodding his head. "She did this? Before she left Prescott?"

Jonathan nodded his head. "She introduced herself to Cooney and spent ten hours going over the contracts and the account books. By the time she reached here, she had enough notes to complete what she had started."

Montgomery was impressed, and he let it show. He replaced the folder, tapping the stiff cardboard with a tobacco-stained finger. "She doesn't have a very high opinion of your brother as a driver, does she?" It was difficult for the man to keep a straight face.

The pencil Jonathan had been toying with snapped. "Her opinion of Coop as a driver isn't the issue, Logan. There isn't a man on the line who could have avoided that kind of accident, regardless of what Miss O'Rourke thinks. After all, driving isn't her field of expertise." He paused for effect, and then continued, "Speaking of experts, I haven't seen your man Delgado around lately, Logan. Any idea where he might be? Or where he might have been the day of the rockslide?"

Montgomery enjoyed playing cat-and-mouse games with Jonathan, but the question about Ramón Delgado unnerved him. He supposed it was Jonathan's training as a lawyer. He exhaled loudly and answered Jonathan's question with a question of his own. "You aren't suggesting that I had anything to do with that accident, are you?" A benign smile pulled at the corners of his mouth.

"I'm suggesting that your man Delgado isn't in town. I'm also reminding you that I know how you've dealt—how Delgado has dealt—with other people when you've wanted to buy them out. And you want the Dundee Transport Line. . . ."

Montgomery smiled coldly. "I thought we were friends, Jonathan," he cajoled. Assuming an air of injured innocence, he lifted his shoulders in a weary gesture of resignation. "Besides, I told you in the beginning that we'd handle this entire matter your way. As long as I get what I want, I'm not going to be concerned about the how or the why."

*   *   *

The first rest stop was at the way station midway between Phoenix and Casa Grande. As run by Adam Becker and his assistant, Mick Flynn, the depot offered little in the way of comfort, but the stop allowed the passengers and driver time to stretch their legs. Estevan was the most appreciative, his stomach still rebelling from the copious amounts of whiskey he had consumed the night before. He engaged in a long love affair with the backyard pump, dousing his head and rinsing his mouth.

"Cinnamon hearts," Cooper suggested, handing the man a dry towel. "You need a mouthful of cinnamon hearts."

Folley laughed. He and Cooper had eaten them by the bagful when they were younger—when neither one of them was old enough to be allowed to drink and both of them were terrified of their fathers finding out. "What I need," he reckoned, "is someone to remind me that a thirty-year-old brain is always attached to a thirty-year-old stomach." He rubbed his still-sore belly. "Promise me we aren't going to do this again, Coop. Not ever."

Cooper nodded. He'd been breaking in a new hat the whole trip, and even that slight pressure had hurt. He was almost sorry that he had given Michael his battered and very soft Stetson. "By the way," he said, his mind following up on the thought, "have you seen Michael?"

Folley shook his head. This time the pain wasn't as intense as it was before. "Not since we ate," he said.

The object of Cooper's concern was exploring the outbuildings behind the depot. He poked and prodded his way through a ramshackle barn, into a dilapidated lean-to, and then along the wire fence to the place where Adam Becker, the stationmaster, kept his cages of gamecocks.

One by one Michael passed their cages, the multicolored cocks rushing the wire and beating their wings as he approached them. The birds were huge and vicious, and the natural spurs that adorned their legs were sharp and daggerlike. Again and again, the birds charged the wire, intent on reaching the boy. He watched them, intrigued by their meanness, entranced by the scars and wounds they bore. Once-proud combs lay flat and shredded against their heads, and more than one rooster was without an eye.

Michael backed away from the cages, afraid the noise would attract the grownups. He'd left the table before they'd finished their meal, excusing himself to use the outhouse and then never going back. He sighed. He'd be in trouble with Regan—but then, he was always in trouble with Regan.

He heard the dog's presence before he actually saw him. The heavy panting sound startled him, and visions of mythological beasts flashed through his mind. It seemed as if the sound was all that was there, the quick *huh, huh, huh,* loud and ominous and seeming to have no worldly origin.

The big animal was black as night itself, invisible against the dark shadows cast by the walls of the three-sided shed. He lay there, watching the boy, his eyes bright as onyx.

Michael held out his hand. He bent down slowly, dropping the stick he held in his right hand, his left extended toward the dog. Warily, he crept closer, his voice a soft singsong as he talked to the animal. He remembered the piece of buttered bread he had stuck in his pocket when Regan wasn't looking and brought it out.

The dog lay still, stretching out his neck to sniff at the hunk of bread. Caution surrendered to the stronger need for food, and the animal's pink tongue gently curled around the proffered morsel as delicately as a baby's finger around its mother's thumb. There was a slow thumping as the dog's tail lifted and fell against the packed dirt. With his nose, he explored the boy's empty hand, the big tongue appearing again to lick his fingers clean. Michael was sorry that he didn't have more.

"Good dog," Michael whispered. "Good dog." He moved closer, still hunkered down, his flat palm stroking the dog's massive head. Impulsively, he began smoothing the tangles at the dog's ears, his fingers raking through the snarls and knots as he gently separated the hairs.

He moved his hand, working down the back of the dog's head, his fingers entwined in the animal's coat. The hair here was longer, thicker, the matting worse than on his head. Inch by inch, the boy worked his fingers through the dark hair until he reached the animal's broad neck.

There was a sudden low snarl, the dog's entire body rumbling in protest to the boy's touch. Instantly the animal's head jerked up and back. The enormous mouth opened, exposing a full set of sharp teeth, and quickly snapped shut.

The boy was held fast, his entire forearm trapped between the big dog's powerful jaws. Michael fell forward on his knees, nose to nose with the animal, and saw the beast's upper lip curl away from the awesome teeth. Tenaciously, the dog held on.

"Michael, where are you?" Cooper's voice called to him from the far yard. Then Regan called, more urgently than Cooper, her voice carrying and seeming to echo. Weakly, the boy called out. "Here!" He watched the dog's eyes and called out again, louder. *"Here!"*

Regan heard the boy's cries. She instinctively knew that something was terribly wrong. Wordlessly, she exchanged a quick look with Cooper, and then together they ran toward the sound.

In spite of her skirt, Regan outdistanced the man. She was a full length ahead of him when they reached the covered lean-to and entered the shed. It took a little time for their eyes to adjust to the darkness. At first, all they could see was the boy and the fact that he was hunkered down on his knees on the dirt floor.

And then they saw the dog, heard the dog.

Cooper was wearing the pistol that was so much a part of his being when he was driving. It seemed to grow from his right hip, and even Regan had not realized the weapon was there. Now, seeing it, she was swept with a sense of relief.

Michael's reaction was different. Wide eyed, he watched as Cooper slipped the Remington from its holster. "No," he begged. His eyes pleaded with the man even more eloquently, a single tear trailing down his cheek.

Resolutely, the boy moved his right arm, lifting the dog's head as he strained to raise the arm even higher. The dog held him fast, the animal's teeth still viselike around the child's forearm. "See," Michael said. "Do you see? He's not hurting me at all."

Cooper nodded. He stood there for a long time, debating his next move, grateful the woman had not panicked. Finally, his mind made up, he holstered the weapon. "Estevan?" He could feel the man behind him, so close that the whispered "Yes" was warm and hot across his neck. "I'll need a rope." He felt a chill at his back as the man moved away.

"What do you want me to do?" Regan's voice was calm, the words coming in a controlled, quiet monotone.

Cooper answered without looking at her. He was already taking off his shirt. "Get ready to grab the boy," he breathed.

He bent down, picking up the stick Michael had carried into the shed. Gingerly, he hefted it in his hand, watching the dog's eyes and ears. The animal was watching him, as well.

Cooper unfurled his shirt and made a sudden, quick move, flicking his wrist, and the heavy, coarsely woven pullover cracked loudly just above the dog's head. At the same time, he smacked the animal's hind leg with the stick. "Now!" he bellowed, charging forward as Regan grabbed the boy's free arm.

The big dog went wild. He released his hold on the child's arm, turning to snap first at the shirt, then at the stick. And then he turned on his attacker.

The dog lunged at Cooper, catapulted up and forward by its powerful hind legs. Both front feet slammed against the man's chest, the dog's fury combining with his weight to topple the man over on his back. Cooper's forearm glanced off the dog's chin, and he felt the searing burn of the animal's teeth as they raked across his elbow. His entire arm momentarily went numb, the bone tingling as a sharp pain shot through to his fingertips and beyond.

He grabbed at the dog's ears, using both hands, the muscles and tendons in his neck and shoulders standing out as he pulled the animal's mouth away from his throat. Slowly, he twisted the sensitive hide on both sides of the dog's head, using pain as a weapon to diminish the animal's brute strength. "The shirt!" He yelled at Estevan, straining to hold the dog immobile above him. "Get the shirt over his head!"

Folley did as he was bid. Together, he and Cooper wrestled the animal to the ground. It took both of them to hold him down and tie his feet.

Cooper sat back on his heels, winded. He wiped his bleeding arm across his forehead, his entire body shaking, the muscles in his back and neck still tense. Flexing his shoulders, he let his head drop forward on his chest and closed his eyes. For a long moment, there was no sound but his breathing.

Another sound came then, the slow, anguished sobs of a small child. The boy's arms went around Cooper's neck, and he tasted the salty warmth of Michael's tears as the boy's cheek brushed across his mouth. He returned the hug, feeling the youngster's heart beating with his own, and then pulled gently away. "We've got a dog to take care of, Mr. O'Rourke."

Together, they examined the big dog. Cooper's neckerchief served as a makeshift muzzle, and the leg ropes remained in place. Gently, Cooper probed at the animal's body, his mouth set in a grim line. He could feel old scars under the dog's thick coat, a row of round knots covering his ribs and belly. Cooper measured the distance with his fingers, swearing bitterly as he realized how badly the animal had been abused. "Pitchfork," he breathed, marking the spaces between the knots with four fingers. "A goddamned pitchfork." Absently, he stroked the dog's neck, meaning to comfort him, drawing back in surprise at the animal's sudden, high-pitched yelp. The dog convulsed, his entire body shaking against the restraints at his feet.

Tenderly, Cooper examined the dog's neck. At the slightest touch, the big animal whimpered, the hide at his neck and shoulders quivering. Steeling himself, the man probed at the thick hair on the dog's neck and chest, his fingers finally closing around a thick, tight strap.

It took considerable time to find the corroded metal hasp. Cooper unbuckled the collar, surprised to find that it did not fall free. And then he knew. He ran his fingers over the piece of leather, counting studded nail heads, realizing at once what they were.

One by one, he worked the half-inch spikes free of the dog's flesh, easing them out of the festering holes. He counted them as he worked, silently, his jaws tightly clenched against his anger. Finally, he was through. He dropped the spiked collar into the dirt at his knee.

"Bring me the water," Cooper said, nodding toward the corner at a bucket kept for the gamecocks.

As soon as Estevan brought it over, Cooper carefully removed the neckerchief muzzle, relieved that the dog did not growl or bare his teeth. Cooper dipped the cloth into the water and gently dabbed at the neck wounds. The animal flinched several times, but made no aggressive movements. When the wounds were sufficiently clean, Cooper carefully tied the neckerchief around the dog's neck, more for show than as a bandage.

Estevan exhaled, his stomach tied in one great knot. "What now, Coop?"

Cooper faced the man, for the first time realizing that everyone had been watching him. He winked and smiled at Michael. "We let him up."

"No . . ." Regan pulled Michael closer.

Cooper's response was subdued, the usual sarcastic humor

gone. "It'll be all right, Regan." He picked up the spiked collar and briefly displayed it before tossing it away. "If that animal was vicious—really vicious—Michael would have been dead when we got to this shed."

The woman felt Michael slip from beneath her fingers. She watched him go, the same feeling in her stomach as when she first found him with the dog. *"Please, God,"* she breathed.

Cooper let the boy help him. Gently, they loosened the bindings on the dog's feet, Michael petting and soothing the animal as they worked. At last the dog was free.

The animal lay there for a time, as if stunned, the expressive eyes darting from one face to the other, settling finally on the boy. The great, shaggy tail lifted and fell against the ground, once—twice—a third time. And then the dog stood.

The big dog moved his head gingerly, as if testing for pain. He shook himself, stretched forward on the massive front paws, and yawned. For a time, he stood still, his eyes staring past the humans who surrounded him to someplace far beyond. And then he searched out the boy. He sat before Michael, expectant, one great paw lifting to rest gently on the boy's small chest.

Michael's face said it all. Remembering the wounds that festered at the dog's neck, he carefully patted the beast's great head. He knew, if he knew nothing else, that the dog was his.

For the first time, Cooper relaxed, his fingers stiff as he unwound them from the butt of his pistol. He felt Regan watching him, and answered her unspoken question with a subtle nod. Their eyes then met, a flurry of unspoken thoughts passing between them—thoughts that neither one truly understood. Cooper cleared his throat, embarrassed as he realized that he was naked from the waist up. Immediately he felt himself on the defensive, and his ensuing words conveyed his discomfort. "Seventeen minutes," he breathed, taking out his watch. "We're seventeen minutes behind, O'Rourke." Without saying it, he made her feel that this time the burden of guilt was solely hers. Head high, she swept past him and headed for the coach.

Estevan was at Cooper's elbow. He held a bundle in his hand, and he offered it to the man. "You're traveling pretty light, Coop. This is your last clean shirt."

Cooper looked at the old flannel shirt, shaking his head. "Good thing I'm heading home, isn't it?" He slipped into the sleeves and felt a degree more human. "Where's Becker?"

Estevan reluctantly jerked a thumb over his shoulder. "He stayed inside the depot." The Mexican's brow knotted. "Let it go, Coop."

Cooper shook his head. "I'm firing his worthless hide, Estevan." There was no need to explain his reasonings. He stared past his friend, his eyes settling on the big man now sauntering toward him. Patiently, he waited, aware that Regan and the others were still within hearing. "You're through, Becker," he said quietly.

The stationmaster snorted. The wad of tobacco that was nested in his right cheek shifted to the left, and he spat. "You can't fire me, boy," he said finally.

"Like hell I can't," Cooper replied. He spied the grizzled hostler and called out to him. "Mick!" Raising his hand, he waggled a finger at the man, not saying anything until the man joined him. "Becker's through, Mick. How would you feel about taking his place?"

Mick Flynn stood with his mouth agape. Nervously, he scratched at the stub of his left arm. A cripple since age ten, the prospect of a good job with decent pay had never occurred to him. He exchanged a quick look with his former boss, then smiled at Cooper. "I can read and write, Coop. And I can do as much with one arm as that lazy jackass ever thought about doing with two." The man was not bragging; he was simply stating fact.

"Then you've got the job." Cooper's eyes had never left Becker's face. "Check out the team," he ordered gently, knowing that the team didn't need to be checked. Flynn knew it, too. Just as he knew that Cooper wasn't through dealing with the stationmaster.

Cooper waited until Flynn was gone. He took the nub of a pencil out of his pants pocket and relieved Becker of the pad he carried in his shirt. "You give this to Jonathan when you get to Phoenix. He'll give you a draft for what you've got coming. And don't ask him for anything else, Becker—not one thing more." He finished writing and stuffed the pad and note back into the man's pocket.

"You can't fire me, boy!" the sneering man repeated. When Cooper started to walk away, he grabbed his arm. "Malachai gave me this job, sonny! Told me I'd be here till hell froze over, and then some. Fifteen years," he raged. "I been here fifteen years! You fire me and you're makin' your daddy a liar, boy!" he finished.

Cooper faced the man, the color washing from his face. The forced calm was tearing at him, burning a hole in his belly. "Malachai didn't lie, Becker. He just made a mistake. A mistake I mean to correct. You're fired, Becker. Don't make me say it again." He turned, intending to walk away.

"Over a dog!" Becker raged. "Over a goddamned dog!" He grabbed Cooper's arm and made the mistake of taking a swing.

Becker's first blow glanced off Cooper's ear and scraped by his right eye, and Cooper's icy calm dissolved. He charged the man, yielding to his temper, both of them falling to the ground in a flurry of fists and feet.

It was an alley fight, both men landing blows that were meant to punish, to break bone and teeth. Becker planted a well-aimed knee in Cooper's groin, following the blow with a vicious kick that caught Cooper just as he rolled over. The kidney blow stunned him, and he sucked in a great lungful of air, clearing his head against the pain.

Becker scrambled away from Cooper. His hand clawed at the dirt until it closed around the studded dog collar. With a quick flick of the wrist, he wound the piece of leather loosely around his knuckles. He turned and swung, then swung again.

Cooper's mouth filled with blood, the salty taste flooding across his tongue and fueling his own bloodlust. Grabbing Becker's hand, he jerked the leather strap away. Ignoring the frantic pounding of Becker's fists, he pulled the man down, pushing his face into the dirt.

Straddling the stationmaster, he kneed him in the back and grabbed a fistful of hair. With his free hand, he wound the spiked collar around the man's neck and began to pull.

Becker's scream was cut short, the collar tearing into his neck as Cooper gave the strap a vicious, sudden twist. He kept on, intending to kill him, remembering the tortured dog with the festering wounds at his neck, the older wounds on his chest and belly.

"Coop!" Estevan's voice penetrated the black silence. "For God's sake, Coop!" The Mexican's hands tore at Cooper, trying to pull him away.

Cooper swung a fist at his new attacker, still holding onto the collar and kneeling on Becker's arched spine. Estevan was knocked backward, but he scrambled to his feet, charging Cooper a second time.

He grabbed Cooper's long hair, pulling hard. And then, coldly, efficiently, he backhanded his friend—hard, purposely, not holding back.

The single slap sobered Cooper, the madness draining from him. He released his hold on Becker, both hands free now and extended as he fought to regain total control. Slowly, he rose up and backed away.

Beitermann and the others moved in, hauling Becker to his feet and leading him back to the depot, for the first time in the long day involving themselves and no longer just watching.

Estevan dug into his pocket. He handed Cooper his white handkerchief and watched it turn red beneath Cooper's nose. He felt a need to say something, anything. He nodded toward the retreating legislators and forced a smile. "Becker's a potential voter, Coop. A man has to consider that."

Cooper returned the wry smile. Beitermann and the other men had been Malachai's friends. And now that Malachai was dead, they no longer had to pretend friendship with his part-Indian son. "Half-breeds and greasers need not apply. Is that how it is, Estevan?"

Folley's laughter was devoid of any humor. "What took you so long, Coop? I've known that since I was born."

Regan was beside the coach. She had made Michael get inside—Michael and his dog. It was beyond her comprehension, all that she had just seen. There were so many sides to Cooper Dundee. So many sides that she could only guess at; so many that she had already seen.

She thought of him, tender and compassionate with Michael, with the dog—as if there was a capacity for love within him that no one but the boy could reach. And then she thought of him with Becker and the insane way he had vented his rage on the man. She closed her eyes and felt a sudden chill, as if a cloud had passed and obscured the sun. *It's got to stop,* she thought. *I'm sorry, Michael, but it's got to stop.*

Chapter 5

The young blond woman stood toward the back of the large room that was the Southern Pacific Railroad Station in Casa Grande. She silently watched as Cooper attended to stage-line business, smiling as he shared an off-color joke with the freight agent. In the two years she had been away, she had forgotten how good looking he was—how, when wet, the dark hair at his ears and collar always curled in the tight ringlets that he hated, and she coveted. He seemed taller now, too, and slimmer than she remembered, but the lithe way he moved—the animal grace that was there even when he was still—was just the same.

She waited, toying with the sculpted ivory handle on her silk parasol, silently ignoring the appreciative stares of the men who entered the waiting room, totally unaware of her own attractiveness as she considered her planned surprise.

Finally, Cooper was finished. He tucked the yellow bills of lading in his vest pocket, his head bowed in such a way that the woman knew she could approach him without being seen. Lightly, she stepped across the room, lifting her skirt in an effort to move even more quietly. She reached him, standing almost toe to toe, and a small puff of white dust rose as she let go of her skirt and let the hem cover her shoes. "Could you help a lady in distress, kind sir?"

Cooper's eyes were fastened on the small feet in front of

his own. He lifted his gaze, working from the bottom up, measuring the cut and color of the woman's gown, her small waist, the curve and fullness of her breasts. "I'd be a fool not to try, ma'am," he breathed.

His gaze shifted to her face then, his eyes locking on the petite features as his next words died in his throat. "Angela?" he murmured finally. "Angela!"

"You're as incorrigible as ever, Cooper Dundee," she scolded. "And just as handsome!"

He swept her off her feet, lifting her up to eye level before planting a kiss on her small mouth. "You playing hookey, little sister, or did the good nuns finally realize you were a lost cause?"

She beat his shoulders with her gloved fists, and then hugged his neck. "Early graduation, big brother. A reward for my natural intelligence and incredible sense of scholastic responsibility." The second hug was more reserved than the first, but as affectionate.

Cooper released her, gently lowering her to the ground. The pride and the affection were obvious in his face and his eyes. "All grown up, Angela." He smiled. "You went away a little girl, and now . . ." He held her at arm's length and was pleased with what he saw.

There was a distinct poignancy in her smile, and her eyes changed. The blue seemed to darken, as if a veil had been drawn over them, and she seemed far away. "I don't think I was ever a little girl, Coop." Old memories escaped the closets of her mind, and she closed her eyes against them.

Cooper shushed her and pulled her close. "Shut up," he groused. He held her for a long time, his chin resting on her flaxen hair. "God," he said finally. "Does Mother expect you?"

Angela's mood changed, and she pulled away, careful to keep her arm around him. "I wanted it to be a surprise, Coop. I wanted to be home for her birthday, and to be there . . ." The smile grew, and there was a rush of color in her cheeks.

Cooper gave her a quick look, and noted the blush. "Estevan," he guessed, elated. "You wanted to be at the ranch when Estevan and the others came through!"

Angela returned his smile. She knew that it would be useless to argue, to try and tell him anything but what he wanted so much to believe. She chose the middle path, not wanting to hurt him. "I'm always glad to see Estevan, Coop. You know that." It was true. Estevan was special. He had always been special and a good friend at a time when she had no friends.

Cooper took her answer as an affirmation of all his own hopes. He'd never once considered anyone else good enough for his adopted sister, just as he had never considered the possibility that there could be anyone else worthy of Estevan. His happiness prompted yet another hug.

Unnoticed, Regan watched the reunion between Cooper and the mysterious and attractive young woman from the narrow doorway that separated the freight office from the main waiting room. There was a stirring inside her, a sudden inexplicable surge of strong feeling that confused and angered her. She felt herself succumbing to a feeling of jealousy, as if she had some claim on Cooper, some interest in him beyond business. Angry, she turned away, leaving the man to his diversions—to his woman.

Logan Montgomery sat in the impressive inner room of his Phoenix office, dominating and dictating the behavior and humor of the men who were with him by his brusque and authoritative manner. They yielded to his demands, shuffling and reshuffling the maps and papers that filled the tables and spilled onto the carpeted floor, nodding their heads at his suggestions, listening carefully to his evaluations.

Red lines scored the large maps, surveyors' notations logging the measurements in degrees and rods, the proposed railroad routes bisecting the territory in a long line running north and south. "Here," Montgomery declared, his finger poking against the stiff parchment. "I want the estimates for a spur line that would have access to the main."

Ramón Delgado knew the place his employer indicated without even looking. There was no need for him to look or question as the others were undoubtedly but silently questioning. It was Malachai Dundee's sprawling acreage south of Casa Grande. Or more properly, all that remained of the once vast Delgado-Esperanza land grant—his family's land grant.

The Mexican smiled, watching Montgomery over the bent heads of the others. There was no rancor in his face, only the sardonic understanding of a man who could feel an affinity for another man's needs, another man's thirst for power and wealth. It was, of course, ironic that he could be so charitable in his feelings, but then Montgomery was going to achieve what Delgado had only dreamed: Montgomery was going to take the *rancheria* as generations of Anglos had always managed to take what they wanted—as they had taken the land from Delgado's father: through deceit. Deceit and, if need be, murder. The thought of someone—of some gringo— dying made Delgado smile.

He was roused from his pleasant and gruesome fantasies by the slamming of a door. Montgomery had dismissed his underlings and had sent them on their way. Delgado knew that the end of the first meeting was only the beginning of the second. "And now, *patrón*," Delgado smiled.

Montgomery studied Ramón Delgado for a long time before he answered his lieutenant. "You did a sloppy job, Ramón." He paused, watching the mercenary's impassive face. "The only thing you accomplished with that rockslide was a minor accident that didn't—" he gave a weak wave of his hand "—amount to a pile of horse crap."

The Mexican's smile didn't change. He rolled a brown- papered cigarette and lit up before he responded. The words came with a steady string of blue smoke, his voice strained, somehow different, as if he were more concerned with retaining the smoke than with talking. "You said no killing, *patrón*." The smile grew. "For now," he finished.

Montgomery recognized the acrid scent of wild hemp. "For now," he echoed. He smiled. "I'm going to make Dundee a final offer." He beckoned for the man to help him and began rolling up the maps.

"For the stage line or for the land?" Delgado asked. He already knew the answer.

"For the line *and* the land," Montgomery answered, thinking he would own it all—the rights-of-way, the Dundee ranch, the railroad. And when Phoenix became the capital— and one day the city would—he would call the tunes while the others danced.

"And if he won't agree to sell?" Delgado's hands were busy, the long fingers working at one of the red-lined maps. He rotated the paper until it formed a tight, solid core.

"Then we'll have to think of something to make him change his mind, won't we?" Montgomery's mouth opened in a wide grin, and he began to laugh.

A sharp tapping on the door changed his mood. He scooped the entire bundle of remaining maps up from his desk. "Put them in there," he whispered, indicating the other room with a curt toss of his head as he handed the maps to Delgado. His next words were directed at the person beyond the door. "A moment," he called. "Just a moment!" Delgado disappeared into the adjoining room and just as quickly returned. "Now," Montgomery ordered as he took his seat behind his desk and busied himself with the notepad.

Delgado answered the door, opening it wide and hesitating just a moment before he stepped aside. The benign smile remained the same as before, pasted across his mouth and not touching his eyes. "Mr. Dundee," he said finally. He made an arrogant half-bow and moved out of the way, gesturing with his arm.

Jonathan felt an uncomfortable chill at his back as he

passed Delgado and tried, unconsciously, to shrug the feeling away. He forced himself to ignore the Mexican. "Logan," he greeted, extending his right hand.

The handshake was reserved, perfunctory. Montgomery did not rise. "Sit down, Jonathan." An expert at the subtle art of unnerving a man, Montgomery did not look up. He kept himself busy, making notes on his yellow pad, adding up rows of figures that meant nothing. Finally, he flipped to a clean page and wrote a series of bold, black numbers across the entire sheet. He underscored the amount, twice, and then turned the tablet around and thrust it across the desk.

Puzzled—wary—Jonathan picked up the pad. Unable to conceal the surprise, he inhaled, and the silence was broken by the sudden intake of air. The paper read five hundred thousand dollars—five times the amount he had demanded, and ten times what the line was presently worth. Composing himself, he pushed the pad back across the desk and waited.

"That's my last offer, Jonathan," Montgomery said flatly. "For the line—" there was an intentional pause as he watched the younger man's face "—and for all the property south of Casa Grande."

Already, Jonathan was shaking his head in disbelief. "The original deal was a hundred thousand dollars for the line and the rolling stock, with options on the rights-of-way." Unspoken by Jonathan was Montgomery's assertion that when the railroad came, they would be partners.

"I've changed my mind," the speculator declared. He leaned back in his chair, drumming the pencil against his desktop. Delgado smiled at him from behind Jonathan's back, and Montgomery found himself wishing for the old days, when a single bullet to the brain ended a property dispute. "You'll retain an interest in the line—in the right-of-way," he said, "just as before. But . . . I need the house at Casa Grande." He leaned forward in his chair. "I *want* the house at Casa Grande."

Jonathan wiped his hand across his mouth. He wanted a

drink and some time to think this through. He stalled, carefully rehearsing the words before he spoke them. "This is premature, Logan. Even the sale of the line is still an uncertainty, an intangible." He stared up at the ceiling.

Montgomery snorted, refusing to play the game. "Bull!" The swivel chair squeaked loudly as he shifted his weight and leaned back. "Ever since Malachai died, Jonathan, you've intended selling the line. It represents a loss to you—a big red blot on your otherwise tidy set of books." The man could see that he had struck a nerve. "You're no fool, Jonathan," he cajoled, his tone suddenly paternal. "You're as aware as I am that the line has no lasting potential, and very little real worth beyond the rights-of-way." He pointed his pencil at the younger man and intoned, "In five years, you'll be a drowning man, and the line will be a brick around your neck. If you don't act now—" he emphasized his point, thumping the pencil hard with each word, "—*right now,* you're going to lose it all trying to stay afloat."

Jonathan's mind raced as he weighed the options that were open to him. He needed Montgomery, just as he needed Montgomery's money. His future—the political future he planned as governor—depended on the man's continued goodwill and backing. He rose up from his chair and began pacing, hoping for a compromise. "Right now my hands are tied," he said finally, facing Montgomery. He lifted them, as if displaying his fetters, and continued. "It's one thing to convince Coop and Teresa to sell the transport line—I'm sure Miss O'Rourke's report will verify that the line is an inefficient operation." His brow knotted and his voice changed as he forced himself to think of the woman. "But to convince them that the ranch should be sold . . ." Bitter, he shook his head and felt a swell of rage, thinking, *Malachai's damn will!*

"My hands are tied," he finally repeated. "Neither one of them will ever agree to sell the ranch." He wondered now if that wasn't why Malachai had changed his will—why he had decided to make definite legal provisions for Teresa.

Montgomery was drawing circles on his notepad—large circles at first, spiraling them inward and making them tighter, smaller. "What about Angela?" he asked, beginning again. He was vaguely familiar with the details of Malachai Dundee's will, with the scandal that had been whispered about when the document was finally probated: Malachai had left equal shares of his estate to his common-law half-breed wife and his bastard quarter-breed son. But he wasn't sure about the girl, Angela, the foundling Malachai had brought home for his woman to raise when the child had been found alive after the 1871 massacre of the Apaches at Camp Grant north of Tucson. "Does the girl have a share of the estate?"

Jonathan's face softened briefly. He shook his head and silently cursed his father's strange sense of fairness and total lack of propriety. "No," he said, answering the other's question without fully understanding his interest. Montgomery signaled for Delgado, and Jonathan watched as the Mexican poured two drinks. He accepted the glass without looking at the man. "Malachai left Coop . . . Teresa . . ." the woman's name rolled off his tongue like a swear word, ". . . and me one-third shares of everything. Everything." He drained the glass, rolling it between his palms.

Montgomery's mind was working. His eyes narrowed and he measured Jonathan's words against what he knew about Malachai and his stubborn determination about what was right. He couldn't believe that the man had died without making some provision for the Anglo child he had brought into his home and raised as his own daughter, unless . . . "Tell me," he prodded, "what would happen to Teresa's share if something happened to her?"

"It would pass to Angela," Jonathan answered without thinking. The meaning of his words—their significance—eluded him.

They did not escape Montgomery's shrewd mental scrutiny. He smiled inwardly and exchanged a fleeting glance with an equally aware Delgado. He nodded covertly at Jonathan's empty glass and waited until Delgado had refilled it a second time, and then a third. He was careful to keep his tone conversational. "How old is the girl now?" he asked. He drained his own glass and sat it upside down on his desk. "I mean, did you ever really find out just how old she was? Where she came from?"

They were familiar questions, and Jonathan had no reason to suspect Montgomery's curiosity. He considered the diversion an advantage he didn't want to lose. He needed to buy some time, while keeping Montgomery's interest in purchasing the line alive. He thought of Angela as she was eight years ago—the tiny, frail, and wounded little girl that Malachai had brought home from the slaughter at Camp Grant.

"She was just twelve. Her parents—her real parents—didn't want her," he confided. A fleeting, bittersweet memory touched him, and he recalled his surprise when Angela was finally scrubbed clean and the stink of the Apache washed off her. It was hard, even now, to imagine anyone not wanting her, to realize that—out of stupidity and fear—her own parents had refused to take her. She had looked like a doll, a fragile, cerulean-eyed doll with long wheat-colored hair and a frightened, delicate face. "Malachai made all the arrangements with her family and brought her home." He said the final word without realizing it, the brandy mellowing the old bitterness.

Montgomery watched as Delgado filled Jonathan's glass again. *So*, he mused, silently ciphering, *the girl is only twenty.* . . . "Your father's will," he coaxed. "Who was named executor of it?"

Jonathan was no longer thirsty. He stood up and placed the still-full glass on Logan's desk, declaring, "I'm the executor." That much, at least, had stayed the same.

Montgomery rose from his chair. Silently, he acknowledged Malachai's wisdom. The old fox had given Teresa a third, knowing, because of her age, she would survive long enough to act as the glue that would hold his sons together—

hold his empire together. She would have the final word in everything, siding with Cooper—or with Jonathan—whenever the need arose, but forever preserving the traditions and the goals that Malachai himself had dictated. The old fox was still running the business from his grave.

Montgomery reached out and placed his hand on Jonathan's shoulder, carefully appraising his face. He said softly, "The girl is only twenty." There was a quiet hesitation as he waited—hoped—for Jonathan's understanding. "If something happened—" the effect of his next words was carefully calculated "—to your stepmother, you'd have control of a two-third majority share. Angela is a minor, Jonathan. If something happened to the squaw, the girl would become your ward."

He lifted Jonathan's glass from the desk and drained it, saluting the man. "You could sell it all, Jonathan—the line, the land—and Coop couldn't do a goddamned thing."

Jonathan tilted his head, studying the man's face, his stomach doing a slow roll as he began to comprehend Montgomery's reckonings. "No," he breathed. He shook his head slowly, and then more vigorously. "No!" Watching Delgado out of the corner of his eye, he shook a long finger at Montgomery. "You're suggesting murder, Logan!"

Montgomery leaned his bulk against the big desk and folded his arms across his belly, still facing Jonathan. A bucolic smile appeared. His tone was affable and innocent. "I was merely speculating, Jonathan. Just presenting a simple 'what if.' You put a name to it, boy." The man reached out, his rigid index finger thumping hard against Jonathan's broad chest. *"You!"*

Jonathan knocked the man's hand away. "Logan, I'll sell you the line. But nothing more. I won't even ask Teresa and Coop if they would be willing to sell anything more." His own smile was as sincere as the other's.

It was a standoff, and Montgomery knew it. He had tried, and he had failed—for the moment. "I told you that I want it all, Jonathan,'' he reiterated. ''The line *and* the ranch at Casa Grande.''

Jonathan shook his head. ''You *want* the land, Logan. But you *need* the transport line.'' He pulled himself erect, feeling in control for the first time since entering the room. ''I told you when we first talked, Logan. I'll get you the line. But *my way,* and in my time.'' He turned so that he could see Delgado as well. ''My way,'' he repeated.

Montgomery's mood seemed to change, and he laughed, pretending that none of it really mattered. ''Can't blame a man for trying, Jonathan. You've known me long enough to realize that I had to give it a try.'' He offered his hand, as if he were accepting Jonathan's terms as final. ''It's the horse trader in me,'' he cajoled.

Jonathan took Logan's hand, still wary. ''One hundred thousand dollars,'' he murmured. ''For Dundee Transport and an option on the existing rights-of-way.'' He felt a real need to clarify the limitations.

Montgomery nodded. ''Win a few, lose a few,'' he demurred philosophically, pumping Jonathan's hand with renewed vigor. ''You're like your old man. Stubborn, shrewd—but honorable.'' He managed to say the words as if he meant them to be complimentary.

He watched as Jonathan took his leave, staring at the place he had stood long after the door had closed between them. Finally pushing himself away from the desk, he joined Delgado, staring out the window and following Jonathan with his eyes as the man crossed the street and headed for his office.

''I want to get rid of Teresa Dundee,'' he finally intoned.

Delgado fingered the painted trim at the window's edge, tracing the wood strips that separated the glass. The Mexican tapped at the window pane and nodded in the direction of Jonathan's office. ''He could make trouble.'' He changed his mind. ''He *will* make trouble.''

"He'll sell me the land," Montgomery smiled. "After she's dead, he won't have any choice."

Delgado was unconvinced. "He'll know that we did it, Logan. And he'll turn us in."

Montgomery shook his head. "The woman is going to die, Ramón." He raised a finger and traced a hangman's noose in the dusty glass, and the stick image of a strangled man dangling from the loop. A second and third macabre image joined the first as he continued speaking. "And if you and I hang, we'll all hang together, my friend. Because if he says one word—if he makes one accusation—I'll convince this whole town it was his doing, his idea. There isn't a man between here and Tucson that doesn't know how Jonathan feels about the woman."

There was a chilling silence as he considered his own words, then came the sound of his equally frigid laughter. "One word, and I'll have the whole world believing that Jonathan Dundee arranged for the woman to die. . . ."

The stagecoach was still at Casa Grande, awaiting the final loading of the mail in the boot—and the loading of Michael's dog up top.

Regan had finally agreed to Michael's riding with the driver. In fact, she was almost relieved when the young woman who had joined them protested riding with the dog inside the coach. And now they all stood watching as Cooper, Michael, and Estevan tried to coax the beast aboard.

Forgetting the boy, Estevan swore. "Damn! Shoot him, Coop," he grimaced, trying to corral the animal long enough to get his arms around him. "He'll be a lot easier to load if he's dead!"

Michael's outraged cry cut through the man's complaints, and the dog began to bark in chorus. Cooper grabbed the boy before he delivered a well-aimed kick at Estevan's unprotected shins. He tucked the boy under his arm and held him fast.

Spying a wide plank that leaned against the platform railing, Cooper rallied. With the boy still cradled against his hip, he lifted one end of the board and dragged it to the side of the coach. "You," he ordered, righting the boy, "get your little fanny up there." He hoisted the boy into the driver's box.

Both hands now free, he jimmied the plank into place and wedged the base firmly against the station platform, the other end resting on the side rails on the driver's seat. Satisfied, he dug into his shirt and pulled out a long piece of dried beef he had been saving for the boy and broke it in half. One piece, he offered bit by bit to the dog. The other, he handed Michael. "Show him the meat, son."

The dog nuzzled Cooper's hand first, searching for more meat there, and then lifted his nose to test the air. "Here," Michael coaxed. He tapped the board with the stiff piece of beef. "Here. . ."

The big dog stepped onto the makeshift ramp, felt it give beneath his weight, and backed away. Nervously, he danced at the foot of the board, lifting a paw as if ready to climb, and then hesitating. Michael leaned forward, stretching out belly down on the planking as he waved the piece of dried beef in front of the dog's nose. "C'mon, boy," he begged. "Please. . ."

Trust and hunger combined to urge the animal forward. He scrambled up the planking, helped along by Coop's steadying hands, and climbed over the handrails into the seat. "Nothing to it," Cooper lied as he kicked the board free, dropping it into the dirt.

Estevan was unimpressed. "And when we get where we're going, Coop, how do we get him off?" He stood there, hands stuffed into his pockets, delighting in his role as devil's advocate. Visions of the dog and Coop growing old together in the driver's seat prompted a soft chuckle.

"Go to—" Cooper spied the women, and caught himself,

swallowing the rude order he had intended just for Estevan's ears "—your seat," he finished.

Estevan shook his head. "After I've helped the ladies," he grinned, eagerly turning and heading for the side of the coach, his laughter echoing in the air.

Chapter 6

Aaron Beitermann and his three legislative associates had succeeded in effectively segregating themselves from the two women, commandeering forward and middle benches. The four men sat facing each other, two on either side of a makeshift lap table, a deck of playing cards their prime concern.

Regan O'Rourke shifted in her seat in an attempt to ease the cramping in her long legs, turning and pressing one shoulder against the window frame as she settled sideways into the lightly upholstered seat. The move had been calculated, and she made it as much for her comfort as in an effort to appease her growing curiosity about her companion.

She studied the young woman's profile. It amazed her, the degree of innocence she found there. The woman was also awesomely attractive in the petite way that men found so captivating—as Cooper Dundee had obviously found her so captivating. . . .

Regan cleared her throat, her eyes shifting to the slim volume the young woman was reading. "It must be very good," she began. Angela's eyes lifted, and Regan continued. "I'm sorry," she apologized. "It's just that you seem to have succeeded in losing yourself completely, as if you were sitting somewhere far away from all this. . . ." She waved her hand at the cloud of blue cigar smoke that hovered in the air between them. "It makes me envious, and I wonder if you would permit me to borrow it when you are through."

"It's actually a gift." Angela closed the book and held it up for Regan's inspection. "For my mother." The smile was slow in coming, but as it grew, it wrinkled the skin at the corners of the young woman's eyes and warmed them. The warmth faded slightly as she stared past Regan to where the four legislators sat huddled over their cards, and her voice lowered. "I didn't learn to read as early as most other children," she whispered. "But when I did, it was as if there weren't enough books printed to fill my needs."

She laughed—a pleasant sound that came from deep within— and lovingly stroked the leather cover of the book. "My mother had a book of poems. I read them over and over, until the binding wore out and the pages came loose. This book," she breathed, "was meant to replace the other. And I'm about to wear it out, too." She closed it and held it pressed between her palms, as if testing her willpower.

"We could talk," Regan suggested.

"About Coop and me?" Angela answered. She canted her head, still smiling, and looked much older and wiser than she had looked before.

"Is my curiosity that transparent?" Regan's own smile mirrored her embarrassment. She leaned forward, the nagging resentment she had felt when she first saw the young woman replaced by a genuine feeling of concern. "Have you known him a long time?" she asked gently.

Angela nodded, biting her lower lip in order to suppress the smile. "Long enough," she answered.

Regan's right eyebrow raised, and she explored the girl's face, carefully contemplating her next words. "I'm sorry," she began. "It's just that . . ." The hesitation came out of frustration—not knowing how to proceed. She scolded herself mentally. Aloud she said, "He seems to care for you, and you seem to care for him; but . . ." She inhaled and plunged on, determined to get it said. "But . . ."

"He's my brother," the girl interrupted. This time she didn't bother to hide the smile. "I'm Angela Dundee," she said, extending her hand.

Thoroughly embarrassed, Regan collapsed against the back of her seat, her hand covering her mouth as she began to laugh. "I feel like such a fool! I saw you—this sweet, quiet young woman—and thought of all the things I know about Coop, all the things I've seen in the past few days. . . ." Her mood changed, and she touched the girl's hand. "I know it was wrong of me, but I really felt like I had to say something—to *do* something."

Angela withdrew her hand. She had sensed the animosity between her brother and this woman when they were at Casa Grande, but Angela's questions to Cooper had gone unanswered. A portion of this antagonism was undoubtedly his own fault, but he was now under attack, and she felt a sibling's need to defend him. "Coop is a good man," she announced. "A gentle man . . ."

Not wanting to alienate the young woman any further, Regan skillfully changed the direction of their conversation. She sighed, "If he were only more like Jonathan. . . ."

Angela's pale eyelids fluttered, and she felt a sudden tightening in her chest, as if someone had touched her heart. "You know Jonathan?"

Regan's smile was reflective, and she nodded her head. The memory of their first tense meeting warmed her, and she laughed. "He's a fine man, Angela," she said finally. "A dreamer . . . but a practical dreamer." For some reason she felt a need to make that distinction. "The kind of man that would make a woman feel safe—and proud of his accomplishments. He's going to be a very important man someday, Angela." Without realizing it, she had said the words as if she were trying to convince herself that it was true. "An important man who really cares about the people around him." She recalled his words: "Someday, Regan, I'm going to be governor."

Angela's appraisal of Regan's face was covert and thoughtful. She searched for a flaw—any flaw—and was wise enough to admit she could not find one. This was the kind of woman that Jonathan wanted: someone poised and beautiful; someone closer to his own age, with the maturity and grace that was required of a woman of social prominence; someone whose past could bear the scrutiny of Jonathan's friends and associates without scandal and shame. . . .

Camp Grant. Angela inhaled sharply, her hand going to her throat as the memories engulfed her. The sharp aroma of the thick smoke from Beitermann's cigar became one with the remembered smell of gunsmoke, and she saw the crimson horror and fury of the massacre again. She felt herself being suffocated under the dead weight of an old woman's body, and then the other pain swept her—the soul-wrenching pain she had felt when her real parents denied her.

They had come, long after the "battle," with all the others who came to look for their lost children among the white captives who had survived. But they left Angela behind. They picked up her little brother—the younger brother who had shared her captivity but not her slavery—turned their backs on her, and never once looked back. . . .

Concerned, Regan reached out, her fingers touching the young woman's pale cheek. "Are you all right?" There was no answer, and she tried again. "Angela, are you all right?"

The young woman swallowed. She nodded weakly and fought to compose herself. "I should have known better than to ride sitting backwards," she finally said, making a valiant attempt to smile.

Regan sensed it was a poor lie. She was gratified when she felt a subtle change in the swinging rise and fall of the coach as it teetered up and down on the leather thoroughbraces, and knew that they had begun to slow down.

Angela felt the change, too. "Home," she smiled, her color beginning to return to normal. "I'm home."

*   *   *

Ramón Delgado had returned to the shadow-world that existed beyond the red-brick and wood-sided buildings in the Anglo section of Phoenix. Although he was more comfortable among the Spanish-speaking poor who lived here, he held a secret contempt for these people, despising the way they were content to toil for the white man's pennies on land that was rightfully theirs. Many of them were his blood kin, and yet he felt superior to them. They had sold themselves into bondage, living on the fringes of a society that used them and would someday throw them away. "But not me," Delgado mused smugly. "Not me."

Montgomery needed him. Not the way the other gringos needed the *peones* who tilled the soil and harvested the crops. Montgomery needed his brains, not his brawn; just as he needed his very special skills.

The Mexican chose a table in the far corner of his favorite cantina and sat down facing the door. The crumbling adobe building, whose debris and litter of a quarter of a century compressed into the dirt floor and formed a thick carpetlike mat, had served many purposes over the years. Now it was a place where men came to sate a thirst that originated in the mind and the hungers of the flesh. The whores were young, second-generation ladies of leisure more child than woman, who moved among the tables plying their trade as innocently as the street children begged for coins. Delgado watched them, taking a perverse pleasure in their suffering and relishing the fear he saw in their faces when he touched them.

His game was interrupted as Breed Tatum and Benito Chavez joined him, and he called for another bottle. The two men remained standing, observing the strict amenities Delgado demanded. They were his lieutenants, his *segundos*, men who—although he pretended otherwise—worked *for* him, not *with* him.

He smiled expansively and gestured for them to take their seats. *"Hermanos. . ."*

Brothers. In spirit, if not in fact. These men were mercenaries. Trained by the military, they had failed to adjust to the pomp and circumstance functions of a peacetime army or the rigors of barracks discipline. So they had deserted, taking their skills and their weapons, seeking out the speculators and carpetbaggers who came west after the Civil War—merchants in death who sold their guns to the highest bidders. Like Montgomery and all the rest who paid other men to do their sinning.

Breed Tatum, the dark half-breed, was the first to speak. He was small, compact, a man inside a boy's body that never seemed to age, and there was a beguiling roundness to his face. "It's been a long time, *compadre*. For some of us, too long." He caressed the rawhide-bound handle of his knife as he spoke, pacified by the feel of leather beneath his fingers.

Delgado laughed and leaned forward in his chair, his elbows on the table. His eyes scanned Tatum's smooth face and then shifted to Chavez's lined and furrowed one. Finally he said, "We have business tomorrow—south of Casa Grande."

Chavez grunted, nodding his head. "Casa Grande," he mumbled, pouring another drink.

Tatum laughed. He raised his glass, touching the rim to Delgado's, and the smile grew. "Will we be calling on the widow Dundee?" There was a perversity in his laughter, the kind a boy makes when he has found a gullible victim for a particularly cruel practical joke.

Delgado's hand stroked the younger man's cheek, the caress turning into a playful slap as he murmured, "Tomorrow the drunken Apaches will make a visit to the Dundee *rancheria*."

Regan stepped from the coach, temporarily blinded by the intense light of the afternoon sun. She found herself at the doorstep of Teresa Dundee's home—and was unable to conceal her surprise.

It was as if the house had been transported from another time, another place. The hacienda was of native adobe; the individual foot-thick bricks were mortared together in walls that measured three feet in depth, with the outer walls finished in stucco that had been whitewashed to reflect the desert sun. Clay *botijas* hung suspended from rough-hewn rafters, the water evaporating and cooling the air on the broad patio that extended across the entire front of the house. There was a genteel majesty to the place, an essence of tranquillity that reached out and touched Regan and filled her with a warmth that had been too long forgotten.

Teresa Dundee came as the second surprise. Standing at the doorway, she was unlike anything Regan had imagined. Her clothes, the way she wore her hair—there was nothing to conjure up the image of the squaw that she had perceived when Jonathan talked about his father's half-breed wife. She was tall and lithe, her bearing much the same as her son's. Graciously, she extended her hand, her head tilted as she smiled and read the younger woman's face. "Miss O'Rourke," she greeted gently. The name seemed to roll off her tongue, a subtle accent softening the *R*.

Regan returned the woman's smile. She found herself immediately attracted to Teresa's genuine warmth and the simple directness she saw in the woman's green eyes. There was a brief, awkward pause and then a vigorous exchange of handshakes. Regan smiled. She turned slightly and gestured toward the coach. "Mrs. Dundee, I'd like you to meet a friend," she began. "A good friend. . ."

Angela Dundee reached out, steadying herself as she accepted Regan's hand. She came into the sunlight, struggling to maintain her composure and grateful that Regan had joined in her ruse.

Teresa's smile broadened. She gathered the young woman in her arms, drawing her close in an expansive hug. Over and over, she murmured Angela's name, cradling the girl's head against her breasts. Finally—reluctantly—she released her child, still firmly holding one hand in her own, as if she were afraid that if she let go, the girl would disappear. Then she faced her son. "Cooper. . ."

Regan watched as Coop's face changed. The harshness, the coldness, gave way to a thinly veiled look of adoration. He raised his hands, palms extended, and shook his head. "I swear, Mother, I didn't know she was coming. . . ." he began.

For a moment, it appeared that the woman was going to speak, as if she didn't really believe that her son was totally without guilt in this wonderful sham. However, she changed her mind; she was happy that her daughter was home, and that happiness was extended to the others. She pointed to the open door of the house and gestured for them to enter. *"Mi casa es su casa,"* she said. "My house is your house."

A mood of relaxed joviality prevailed in the large dining room. Teresa and her serving girl kept the wine glasses filled, and the table was spread with the choicest delicacies from the kitchen and storeroom. Aaron Beitermann, Lester Moorhouse, Jarrod Kilmont, and Orrin Pryor were no longer nameless or distant entities, and Regan was at once amused and amazed by their sudden transformation. The degree of congeniality was in direct proportion to the wine the men had consumed; the more they drank, the more friendly and agreeable they became.

Even Michael seemed content. A well-used child's chair and table had been resurrected from a back bedroom, and Teresa and Cooper spent a full five minutes in an animated discussion as to just where the boy would sit. Teresa allowed her son to win the argument, pleased at his obvious show of affection for the child, and watched with her heart as well as her eyes as Cooper placed the table and chair near the open door. It was a good place for the boy, and his chair had been arranged in such a way that he could watch the activity outside or the adults who sat at the table. The dog, of course, was with him, lying beneath the table at the boy's feet, his pink tongue busy as he picked up purposely dropped tidbits.

Regan watched the dog, still feeling uncomfortable that the animal had become so important to Michael. There was a very genuine fear within her, the memory of the dog's first encounter with the boy still shaping her judgment. Another thing that disturbed her was the almost human way the dog measured anyone that approached him. He would watch them, his black eyes alive with interest as he made his quick appraisal. The majority of those he watched were, like Regan, merely tolerated as necessary but uninvited companions; others were dismissed. But some—like Teresa and Michael— were openly admired. Even Cooper rated a thump or two of the dog's tail, Regan thought dryly—so much for the old saw about dogs being completely infallible as judges of a man's character. . . .

"Of course, I intend to ride!"

Angela's exuberant declaration brought Regan back to the here and now. She realized then that she was the only one still sitting at the table, the cup of coffee in her hand already cold.

Angela was leading the way as everyone marched out the front door. She was wearing a pair of boy's trousers, the long legs rolled up around the vamps of a worn, round-heeled pair of boots. A boy's cotton shirt completed her outfit, the hanging shirttails covering the seat of her britches, and she looked more child than full-grown woman.

All four legislators were in their shirt sleeves now, and their faces were red, more from the wine than the glow of the setting sun. Eagerly pushing and shoving each other, they crowded around the high pole fence that surrounded the stock pen. They watched as the Dundee *vaqueros* filled the corral with an assortment of unbroken horses, the animals kicking and squealing in protest to the prodding and poking hands and fingers that urged them on.

Fascinated, Regan watched as two of the hands separated a small bay gelding from the others, the horse bucking and rearing as he was wrestled away from his mates. The animal made a series of small, stiff-legged hops, carrying his tormentors with him, actually lifting them off the ground as he tossed his head.

Grabbing the forelock, Estevan Folley used his free hand to twist the gelding's ear. He applied a steady pressure, forcing the animal's head down, letting go of the mane just long enough to shove the metal bit against the horse's teeth and then into the animal's mouth. Deftly, he slipped the braided rawhide bridle into place. Still holding onto the horse's ear, he called out, "Got him half tamed, Coop! You ought to be able to handle him now."

Angela pushed ahead of her brother. "Well, if he can't, *I* can," she laughed.

"Like hell," Cooper snorted. He picked up his sister, both hands locked firmly around her waist, and set her out of his way. "Go wash the dishes," he ordered. She responded by planting a well-aimed kick against his shin. He laughed and sprinted away.

Regan watched from the fence, her eyes never leaving the activity inside the pen. Absently, she moved aside to allow Michael a place beside her as she watched Cooper vault onto the gelding's back—inhaling sharply as all hell broke loose.

No longer held fast, the horse began to buck. His head came up and back suddenly, and he appeared to be standing erect on his hind feet. Cooper stayed on, coming forward and wrapping his arms around the animal's neck, then shifting his weight back again as the horse came down. The gelding landed with both front legs rigid, the jolting impact almost unseating the thing that was perched on his back.

Cooper felt the vertebrae in his back compacting as the horse landed. The sensation stayed with him as the animal continued to crow-hop around the small holding pen. He could feel a blister raising on his tailbone, and there was another more intense pain at the base of his skull, but still he held on. His long legs were wrapped around the horse's belly, the muscles knotted tightly as he kept his seat.

Fascinated, Regan continued to watch, dividing her attention between the man on the horse and the other men who were watching. They were behaving like small boys, yelling and swearing, poking and punching one another as they made good-natured bets. "Two dollars on the horse," Orrin Pryor yelled. "Five!" Kilmont and Moorhouse echoed. Beitermann's fist was full of greenbacks. Estevan pulled a gold eagle from his pocket. "Ten says Coop rides him to a standstill."

Beitermann took the gold piece. "Birds of a feather," he grinned. The smile faded as he realized what he had said—and when he realized that Estevan understood what he had implied. He stifled a cough, and turned back to the pens.

Cooper's ride ended as it began, with the little bay rearing straight up in the air, and then coming down. This time, though, the animal landed on its knees. Cooper pitched forward, and it appeared that the horse had finally succeeded in unseating him. But he dug in with his heels, using the animal's long mane to keep his balance, and stayed on. The horse remained in its camellike posture, its sides heaving. Then, cautiously, the gelding rose up until it stood on all four feet, its legs splayed. Its back arched as if the animal was bunching itself for one final buck, but then the tense posture eased. The horse was thoroughly winded, the fight gone.

Cooper slipped off the sweat-soaked bay, leaving behind the imprint of his legs and thighs on the mahogany-colored hide. Affectionately, he rubbed the gelding's foam-flecked neck and removed the bridle.

Following Cooper's lead, each man made his ride. And then it was Beitermann's turn. The man hitched up his pants and somehow managed to work his bulk through the narrow space between the fence railings, goaded on by the insults and laughter of his companions. Filled with a sense of bravado inspired by the abundant amount of spirits he had consumed, he swaggered toward the horse that Estevan Folley had bridled.

Estevan eyed the man. "You can always reconsider, Aaron." He smiled as he relaxed his grip on the animal's ear to make a point, and was lifted clear off the ground as the animal tossed its head and tried to break free.

Beitermann sensed the dare and laughed. "I was riding horses like this when you were still wearing three-cornered pants," he snorted.

As before, the animal was without a saddle. There was nothing to protect the rider from the brutal impact that would come each time the horse landed. In this case, there was no need. No sooner was Beitermann helped onto the horse's back than he was promptly dumped into the dirt. He hit the ground and scrambled to his feet, the horse right behind him. The beast charged the man, his neck extended and teeth bared as he chased him across the corral. For a big man, Beitermann could move. He dove through the fence railings, somehow preserving his dignity as well as his balance. He landed on his feet and stood there, feeling as though he had won. Unable to help themselves, the onlookers dissolved into tearful laughter.

Angela smiled at the man and ducked under the fence. "Now that you have him worn out, Mr. Beitermann, I think I'll try!"

Cooper and Estevan had already recaptured the bronc and were holding the animal, waiting for the next rider. Without realizing who it was, they joined hands, lacing their fingers together, and boosted Angela onto the animal's back.

"Damn!" Cooper and Estevan swore in unison, both of them realizing their mistake at the same time. It was too late. The little bay was already loose and running around the corral.

Angela rode longer than any of them thought possible,

clinging to the animal's broad back, her fingers intertwined in the thick tangle of black hair on the horse's neck. But then the gelding jackknifed, folding up in the middle, its neck arched and nose tucked between the long front legs. Cooper and Estevan were already on their way across the corral when Angela hit the ground.

They picked the girl up, and carrying her between them like a limp sack of grain, they raced across the corral and through the partially opened gate. Once outside, Cooper was torn between wanting to hug her and wanting to spank her.

Estevan interceded. He grabbed the girl, sweeping her up in his arms, and covering her face with loud, wet kisses. "Just think of it, Coop," he teased, letting her go, "in addition to slopping the hogs, feeding the chickens, and raising the babies, she could spend all her spare time breaking the horses. *Madre de Cristo,*" he exulted. "What a find!"

Cooper's temper ebbed, and he gave the girl a hug. "You could have broken your neck, brat," he scolded.

Angela pulled away, her hands knotted on her hips. She was tired of all the teasing and patronizing—the way Cooper and Estevan assumed that she was still a child. "Do you want to see me do it again?"

This time, it was Teresa Dundee who intervened. "No, he does not," she declared. "And neither do I." Tenderly, she put her arm around her daughter and dismissed her son and Estevan with a wave of her hand. "While the little boys continue to play, you and I—" she smiled at Regan, who had joined them "—and Miss O'Rourke, will go discuss politics, religion, and the universal weaknesses of mortal man."

Regan was grateful for the invitation. She had grown tired of watching the game between the men and the animals. Putting her arm around Angela's small waist, she and the women began the long walk toward the house. "I loved it," she smiled, giving Angela a quick squeeze. "Even more, I wish that I had joined you!" She did admire the girl's spunk, the way Angela had defied Cooper and had done as she pleased.

Behind them, she heard the sound of Cooper's soft guffaw and, turning, saw from his face that he had heard her. Cooper was shaking his head, his eyes mocking her even more than his laughter. She angrily turned to Teresa, "Mrs. Dundee," she breathed, "I'd like to borrow a pair of trousers and a shirt. Please . . ."

Angela's gleeful laughter—her approving handclap—was silenced by a single look from her mother. "You don't have to prove anything to Cooper, Regan. Ignore him," Teresa advised. She knew at once that her words had fallen on deaf ears. It was puzzling, the unfathomable something that existed between Cooper and this young woman. The young boy, she knew, was a great part of it. But there was more, something that she did not—could not—fully understand. It was as if they had been lovers long ago and had just met again—and chose only to remember the pain and none of the joy of their past love affair. She reached out, patting Regan's hand. "Ignore him," she said again.

Regan quickly changed clothes, fervently praying to whatever god that might be listening that she not make a fool of herself. She slipped into the denim pants that Angela had brought her, fumbling with the buckle in an attempt to make the waist smaller. Giving up, she adjusted the pants until they rested on her hip bones. The shirt was next, and she buttoned it with a degree of trepidation. The blue chambray was soft against her skin but indecently tight, and she had to leave the top two buttons undone. She fiddled with the collar for a time, and then gave up, concentrating instead on her long hair. It took only a few quick movements to pin it tightly in place.

The men were still standing at the fence when she returned to the corral. One by one, they turned to stare openmouthed as she approached. Her long legs seemed even longer now, the faded denim following the lines of her thighs and calves. The shirt was even more distracting, the thin cotton clinging to the soft, round curves and molding her breasts as effectively as a sculptor's hand.

"Coop." Estevan saw the woman first, and he pulled at his friend's arm to get his attention. He said nothing more than the man's name, as if struck dumb, nodding his head in the direction of the house.

Cooper turned, following Estevan's gaze with his own eyes. "Sweet Jesus!" he breathed. He watched the woman, his mouth agape, unable to take his eyes off her. Moving with the quiet grace and suppleness of a large stalking cat, she was aware that she was being watched, yet there was nothing brazen in her step.

But neither was there any humility. She carried her head high, her shoulders squared and her back straight, her eyes meeting each man's gaze directly. Convinced the woman had read their minds—that she knew what they were thinking and how they had mentally undressed her—they averted their eyes, nervously clearing their throats and shuffling their feet. One by one, they turned back to the corral and to the horses beyond.

Except for Cooper. Their eyes met, a brief fire of unspoken challenge flashing between them as Cooper tried to will Regan away, will her back to the house. Resolute, she kept coming. *Fine*, he thought ruefully. He opened the gate, bowed, and let her pass.

Teresa reached out, grabbing her son's arm. "Stop her, Coop," she ordered.

He lifted his shoulders in a noncommittal shrug. "Lady wants to break her neck, it's no skin off my nose," he lied.

Teresa's fingers closed around his wrist. "I want you to stop her, Cooper. I want you to tell her you're sorry—" she felt him try to pull away and held fast "—sorry that you laughed at her."

"Bull!" he snorted. "I'm not one damned bit sorry!" The

petulance yielded to a son's contriteness; he kissed the woman's forehead and broke away.

Regan was in the center of the pen, carefully examining the milling horses. She felt Cooper at her shoulder and smiled up at him. "That one," she said, pointing. "The one with the pretty little white spot on its forehead." She mocked the man with her voice, just as he had mocked her with his laughter.

"You don't have to do this," he murmured. The horse Regan had chosen was one of the few that hadn't already been ridden; a fractious gelding that had eluded the wrangler's rope. The animal bared its teeth, kicked out with its hind feet, and began snaking its way among the others. Thinking the woman had not heard him, Cooper repeated his words, louder. "You don't have to do this!"

"Like hell," she answered. She helped herself to the gloves Cooper had stuffed in his belt and eased them onto her long fingers.

Angry, Coop barked a single order to one of the hands. "The roan!" He watched, helpless, as the animal—kicking and biting every step of the way—was brought to the center of the small arena. It took three men—Cooper, Estevan, and the wrangler to subdue the horse, and they held him in place just long enough for the woman to mount.

The gelding exploded with the pent-up fury of a wild animal freed from the hunter's trap. Humpbacked, he catapulted into the air, all four feet off the ground. He made a series of short, vicious hops, circling the corral and working dangerously close to the fence, landing with a bone-jarring thud. The woman held on.

In desperation, the horse began to run. He extended his powerful neck, his long tongue working against the bit as he charged the fence. He turned just in time, purposely running close to the pole fence in an effort to unseat the woman and knock her off.

Regan anticipated the gelding's move and shifted accordingly.

She raised her right leg, narrowly avoiding a sure collision with the fence, righting herself when the horse spun away and began to buck again.

She rode him to a standstill, pulling his head around and forcing him into a tight circle with her heels. Once, twice, he circled to the right, and then she released his head, only to pull him up again as she forced him to reverse his turns and to circle to the left.

Satisfied, Regan lifted her leg and slipped off the animal's back. She held on to the reins, leading the subdued animal to the place where Cooper and the others stood waiting. "We have horses in the East, Mr. Dundee," she smiled. She removed the borrowed gloves and stuffed them into Cooper's shirt pocket. "And occasionally we even ride them."

Gingerly, she turned her back on the man. Her whole body ached, but she refused to yield to the pain. Head held high, she walked through the gate, relieved when Teresa and Angela offered her their arms. "Somehow," she said with a smile, "I think Coop'd be much happier if I'd broken my neck."

Teresa laughed, and it was a good sound. She looked back to the place where her thoroughly humbled son stood hat in hand—and laughed again.

Chapter 7

Logan Montgomery stared across the huge desk at his companion, his fingers tented beneath his nose. He was considering every word the man was saying, nodding his head in agreement as Ramón Delgado outlined their scheme.

Delgado finished his drink before continuing. The bourbon burned his throat and made him hoarse. His eyes narrowed and he chose his words carefully. "We'll take the women hostage," he began. "And the boy."

There was a noise as Montgomery pushed away from his desk and stood up. "That'll work. The Apache have been known to take women and children," he said, thinking out loud. Still, he was troubled. "The Dundee woman has to die, Ramón. She has to be *found* dead." He faced his lieutenant, feeling a need to explain, inwardly angry that it was necessary. He was careful to conceal the anger, and his tone was patronizing. "She can't simply disappear. We'll need the body," he finished. "In order for Jonathan to have full control, we'll need the body."

Delgado shrugged. The intricacies of the law bored him. "You'll have your body," he promised. *Many bodies*, he thought to himself. The O'Rourke woman and the boy would die as well—and anyone else who got in his way.

Montgomery poured himself a drink and watched as Delgado refilled his own glass. The more he thought about the ruse, the better he liked it. "You'll make your raid tomorrow morning, just as the stage leaves." The smile came slowly. Aaron Beitermann and the other legislators would be there and would see everything. Four of the most influential men in the territory—he dismissed Estevan Folley, knowing his sympathies lay with the *mestizo* and Mexican population—would witness, be part of, a bloody raid by Apache renegades. The Dundee squaw would die, and four Anglo legislators would swear the Apache were responsible.

He laughed. It was all falling into place. He would have the transport line and the land, and Jonathan Dundee would be in his back pocket. And there was more, so much more. Because after a suitable period of time, while the memory of the raid was still alive, he would approach Beitermann, Kilmont, Moorhouse, and Pryor. He would convince them of the need, enlisting their aid, and they would push for the condemnation of reservation lands. Then his railroading empire would grow even larger, and his power would increase tenfold.

Montgomery drained his glass. He smiled as Delgado rose up from his chair. "I'll take my carriage down to Tucson and wait for word there. I want to be nearby when . . . when I'm needed."

Jonathan's legs ached. He stood up in the stirrups in a vain attempt to ease the cramping and cursed himself for not having had the foresight to rent a buggy.

Not that it would have mattered. It was the same each time he made this trip, even when Malachai had still been alive. No matter what form of transportation he chose, the inner feeling was always the same. Every time he returned to the *rancheria*, every time it was necessary to make the journey, he hated it. Just as he hated the woman, Teresa.

He swore again, feeling the bulk of the dispatch pouch beneath his jacket, and kicked the standardbred mare into a more tolerable canter as the hacienda came into view.

Standing on the patio of the house, Angela shaded her
eyes, staring off into the distance. She saw the man's silhou-
ette against the flat landscape, his image distorted and
miragelike above the flat ground. The hot air rose in shimmering waves, contorting the horse's legs, making it appear that
the animal was floating above the ground. There was no
sound yet, no familiar cadence of shod hooves against packed
clay; man and beast appeared to be colored phantoms on a
daylight haunt.

Gradually, the sound did come, at one with a sense of
recognition. Angela felt her heart swell within her breast, and
she began to wave. Before the others even noticed the rider,
she lifted the hem of her skirt and sprinted across the yard.
"Jonathan!"

He dismounted and let go of the mare's reins. He caught
the young woman as she rushed against him and felt the
warmth of her lips against his neck. "Angela?" he said in
surprise.

She blushed deeply, ashamed at the brazen way she had
flung herself at him—but not sorry. Self-consciously, she
smoothed her dress and took his arm. She was in full control
of her emotions now, at least well enough to curb her
enthusiasm. "I've missed you," she said truthfully. She
brightened and patted his arm. "I've missed everyone!"

He took her hand, the way a much older brother would
take the hand of a small child. His eyes swept the cluster of
people at the corral fence. "Coop said that you wouldn't be
home until September."

She laughed, and the sound was not the sound of a little
girl's laughter. "I wanted to be home for Mother's birthday."
There was brief hesitation as Jonathan's stride faltered and
then resumed. "You forgot," she chided, squeezing his arm.

He *had* forgotten—just as he had always failed to admit
that this yearly celebration at the *rancheria* had always been
Malachai's subtle way of honoring Teresa's place in his home
in front of the honored guests from Prescott. "I did forget,"

he answered. He saw the hurt in the woman's eyes and tried to defend himself; putting his hands on her shoulders, he turned her so that they faced each other. "She's *your* mother," he said softly. "Yours and Coop's. Not mine."

The pain that had shaded the young woman's eyes turned to anger. "Don't tell her that, Jonathan—and don't tell her that you've forgotten." She shook her head when he tried to speak. "I've brought enough gifts so that tonight, after dinner, there will be one present from each of us. Don't spoil it, Jonathan. Please don't spoil it. . . ."

He was about to reply when he saw Regan. Just seeing the woman filled him with enough warmth to encompass the world. Forgetting Angela—and forgetting their small quarrel— he quickly walked over to Regan. Angela felt him slip from her fingers.

Their greeting was restrained, proper. He reached out with his left hand and ruffled Michael's hair without really seeing him, while taking Regan's hand with his right. "Hello, Miss O'Rourke," he smiled.

She returned the smile, grateful that she and Angela had changed clothes after their brief rides. "Hello, Mr. Dundee."

Coop strolled up at that moment and interrupted their reverie. "Any problems, big brother?" he greeted.

Jonathan still held Regan's hand as he replied, "Not at all. Anderson's dispatch for the adjutant at Fort Lowell came about an hour after you left."

Coop held out his hand, taking the pouch. He hefted it in his palm, testing the weight. "Was it important enough that you felt you had to make the trip?"

Jonathan felt a pressure against his fingers as Regan sensed his consternation. "It is your mother's birthday," he answered calmly, just as Teresa joined them.

The older woman saw the flush of embarrassment on Cooper's face. "I thank you for coming, Jonathan." She took his arm, gently leading him away. Regan went with them. Tactfully, Teresa waited until they were inside the house before she asked the question. "And the real reason for your being here, *hijo*?"

Jonathan stood in the middle of the large main room, the *sala*, surrounded by his memories and temporarily overwhelmed. It took a long moment to compose himself. "I think you already know, Teresa," he said finally.

She nodded. There was a short pause as she whispered instructions to the cook and dismissed her, and another as she poured Regan and Jonathan each a glass of wine. "Cooper told me about Regan—Miss O'Rourke," she began. "And why she's here. What he didn't tell me," she breathed, "is that you and Miss O'Rourke are . . ." Her smooth brow furrowed as she searched for the words. Unable to find ones she thought suitable, she faced the young woman. "I want an unbiased opinion, Miss O'Rourke." Their earlier congeniality had no place in this discussion, and she wanted the woman to understand that. "An honest evaluation of my husband's—" it was difficult for her to think of Malachai as dead "—of the stage line," she finished. "Now, and what it will be a year from now."

Regan stared into her glass. Rotating the glass between her palms, she said finally, "A year from now—unless there are some drastic changes in policy and in procedure—the transport service will be bankrupt." She lifted her eyes, meeting the steady scrutiny of the older woman.

Teresa Dundee's shoulders sagged, she closed her eyes, and she seemed to age visibly. There was a long silence during which the woman seemed to be somehow renewing herself, to be calling on some hidden reserve that strengthened her. When she at last opened her eyes, they were again vibrant, alive. "Regan, I need to talk to Jonathan. Alone."

Jonathan started to protest, but Regan nodded her head, relieved that she had been asked to leave. "I gave you an *honest* evaluation, Mrs. Dundee." She searched the woman's face for some sign that she was believed.

Teresa smiled. "I know that, Regan." She touched the

young woman's arm. "I was wrong to think that Jonathan—that your feelings for Jonathan—would influence your judgment." The smile grew, and she tilted her head slightly as she made yet another appraisal. "I don't think anyone—or anything—could influence your thinking . . . could influence *you*." She squeezed the young woman's arm affectionately, leaving the rest unsaid. Regan left them, feeling she had been complimented but not knowing why.

"She has a strong will, Jonathan," Teresa declared. "Perhaps too strong."

"That's not your concern, Teresa." The words were sharper than he intended, but he made no effort to apologize. Beginning again, he said, "Logan Montgomery's made an offer for the line and the rights-of-way. One hundred thousand dollars."

"No," Teresa responded. She turned from him and headed for the kitchen, knowing that he would follow.

Perplexed, Jonathan did. "For God's sake, Teresa . . ." he pleaded. They passed through the broad hallway that led to the old part of the house and entered the big kitchen. This room, too, was part of the original house that Malachai had built for his first wife.

Jonathan hated the room without really knowing why, uneasy every time he had reason to enter it. Unconsciously, his eyes drifted along the far wall, settling finally on the rough-hewn door that led to . . . He remembered suddenly: the room Teresa had lived in when he was small and his mother was still alive. The memories that he had suppressed all these years finally came back to haunt him.

"Jonathan?" Teresa called out to her stepson, alarmed at the look on his face. When he didn't answer, she tried again. "Jonathan?"

He responded without looking at her, his eyes still on the door. "How did you do it, Teresa?" he began. "How did you get Malachai into your bed?"

Stunned, the woman dropped a bowl she had just picked up. Her hands were still shaking as she lifted the shards from the tiled floor. She gathered them in her apron and stood up, her fist knotted against the pale muslin. "We're talking about the stage line, Jonathan," she whispered. "And about Logan Montgomery."

"Do you remember my mother, Teresa?" Jonathan's voice was distant, cold, relentless. "Hair like corn silk," he murmured. "White, white skin, and cerulean eyes." His tone softened. "Like Angela," he declared, understanding for the first time why he had accepted her into the family, why he had never resented her the way he had resented Cooper. "I miss my mother, Teresa. I've always missed my mother."

He finished his wine, his fingers closing around the fragile goblet as the anger took hold of him again. The glass shattered against his palm, and he didn't even feel the pain. "How, Teresa?" he demanded. "How the hell did you manage to steal my father?"

Teresa removed her apron. She laid it on the table, fingering the fabric and unable to think clearly. "I *loved* your father," she said finally. "He *needed* me!"

Jonathan's contempt was obvious. He grabbed the woman's arms and shook her. "My *mother* needed you! She was sick, and Malachai hired you to take care of her!" He spun the woman around until she faced the wooden door. "Do you know how many times I saw father sneak into your room?" He turned her completely around, staring into her eyes, cursing when she returned his inspection without wavering. He swore and shoved her away. "My mother died because of a half-breed whore and her bastard son!"

She slapped him hard across the mouth, as if he were ten years old and had sworn at the table. "You've suddenly remembered it all, Jonathan," she began, her voice quavering. Her hand burned, and her fingers trembled, a sudden rush of shame and pity flooding her heart, her very soul. She reached out, tenderly touching Jonathan's mouth with her fingers, sorry that she had struck him. He looked so much like Malachai—the way Malachai had looked when she first saw him as something more than the man who had hired her to look after his wife. *Like Malachai had looked the first time he came to me.* . . . The bittersweet memory brought a flood of quiet tears.

She rolled up the right sleeve of her dress and took Jonathan's hand in her own. "You've remembered everything but the reason for this," she whispered, tracing the long white scar with his fingers. "Your mother was sick, Jonathan. She had been sick for a long time." She held his hand against the thick tear that reached from her wrist to her elbow. "She tried to kill you that night, Jonathan."

Her fingers locked around his palm when he tried to pull away. Without turning, she nodded toward the dark smudges on the wall behind her, the gray splotches that the whitewash never completely obscured. "After she—" Teresa closed her eyes, trying to shut out the horror "—murdered your sisters." *The twins—Malachai's beautiful ten-year-old twin girls.* She continued, her voice a shallow, sad whisper. "Then she came looking for you. For me." She could see from Jonathan's face that he was remembering, that the long buried truths were coming back, and she continued. "Your father had gone to Tucson to get the doctor. I was afraid to leave you alone in your room, so I took you to bed with me."

She had to stop, the memories pouring back with such great force that she felt the terror all over again. She could hear Eliza's mad screaming, could hear the girls' sudden, terrified shrieks, and the more terrifying silence that followed. Eliza had been covered with blood when she came into the room, and her fingers left long, crimson ribbons on the walls.

"Your mother found us," she began again, her voice soft. "You and Cooper and me." The scar on her arm began to burn clear down to the bone, as if the wound had been reopened.

Jonathan's face was ash gray. He swallowed, his eyes filled with images that had haunted him in nightmares all through his childhood—nightmares he had willed himself to forget during the long years he was away at school. "No more," he breathed. He raised his hands, pushing away the unseen demons that filled the room. The quick flash of sunlight on the small mirror that hung above the bed caught his eye, and he remembered the gleam of another kind of light on cold steel. It was true. Everything Teresa was telling him was true. Just as it was true that Eliza Dundee had tried to kill him, and when she failed, had slit her own throat and bled to death at his feet. . . .

Jonathan sank to his knees and silently wept. His body felt completely depleted, used up, when he finally was able to compose himself. He wiped his eyes and cheeks with his handkerchief, but kept staring down at his shoes, unable to meet his stepmother's gaze.

Teresa inhaled. She forced herself to speak, the words coming slowly, deliberately. "We were talking about the stage line, Jonathan." She reached out to touch his arm, changing her mind when she saw him stiffen; it was too soon, too soon. Her arms folded beneath her breasts, she continued, "Is it that important to you, Jonathan, to make this sale?"

He nodded, still tense and feeling awkward. And yet he could not say the words he should have said—not even a simple *I'm sorry*. Instead, he declared, "The railroad *is* coming. Malachai couldn't stop it, and Coop can't stop it. I want to be part of it, Teresa. I *need* to be part of it."

She understood, because she knew his secret dreams, his political ambitions. And she also owed him. In all these years, not once had he ever told Cooper the truth about his out-of-wedlock conception—that Eliza Dundee was still alive a year after Cooper was born.

"I'll talk to Coop, Jonathan." When he tried to speak, she silenced him with a firm wave of her hand. "You're a good man, Jonathan. You're too much like your father not to be a good man. If you think that this is right—if you think that this is really necessary, no matter what the reason—then I won't stand in your way. And I won't allow Cooper to stand

in your way." Tenderly she reached out, and this time he
didn't pull away. "I'll tell Coop what I've decided after
we've had our dinner."

Michael ran beside the outbuildings in back of the big
house, filled with the puff of pride that all small boys feel
when they have successfully escaped the scrutiny of their
elders. For the second time in two days, the ruse had worked,
and he had run from the house with the hopping gait of
someone who really did have to go, and go badly.

Even Cooper had been fooled. That thought prompted a
small twinge of guilt—enough guilt that Michael stopped his
explorations just long enough to empty his bladder at the
corner of the barn. He did his work artistically, using his
water to write his name against the dry boards, straining for
the final spurt that was necessary to dot the *i*. Then he was
off again, the big dog following after him as he headed for
the pens.

The horses were gone now, turned out to forage in the
barbed-wire-fenced pastures beyond the stock barn. There
was a new animal in the corral now, a brindle-faced range
bull Cooper and Estevan had roped out on the range. The
small bull was a throwback, an unbranded maverick that had
survived in the maze of canyons and gullies abutting the
eastern shore of the Santa Cruz River. Short bodied and long
legged, the animal had the gaunt look of the Texas longhorn.

Michael climbed the fence, poking his head through the
rails as he watched the animal from a safe perch. The spotted
bovine returned the boy's slow inspection, contentedly chewing on a mouthful of timothy grass. It looked docile now, a
far cry from the wild and terrifying beast Cooper and Estevan
had driven and dragged into the enclosure, anger and fear no
longer firing the chestnut red eyes.

The boy wanted a closer look. He debated with himself,
his chin resting on crossed arms as he measured the creature.
Covertly, he let his feet slip from the bottom rail, his legs

poking through the fence as his toes came to rest on the dirt inside the corral. Half in and half out, he watched the scraggly runt, just as the bull watched him.

Michael slipped into the corral. He stood for a time, one hand on the fence, remembering what he had seen when Cooper and Estevan had worked with the animal. It had been a frightening game, both men goading the bull, playing the matador to the cheers and jeers of the others. The animal had responded in kind, charging its tormentors, tearing about the corral in a frenzy of dust and debris as it tried to pin them to the fence or the ground.

The boy wiped his nose with his sleeve. "Shouldn't a teased you," he whispered. "Nice cow . . . nice old cow." He began a slow approach, head on, his hand extended as if offering a treat.

The huge black dog remained outside the pen, but now began to whine, pacing up and down in a frantic half-run, his body close to the ground. His dark eyes were riveted on the boy's back, and he scented the musklike smell of the bull that lay heavy on the still air. The dog's neck hairs bristled as he sensed a subtle change in aroma and a series of short, explosive snorts burst from the animal inside the pen. The bull's ears came forward, its nostrils distending as it made the sounds again and dropped its massive head.

Growling, the big dog snaked through the bottom two rails and lunged forward. He collided head-on with the charging bull, the loud noise of bone smashing against bone thundering like the crack of a large-bore pistol. The dog's teeth tore into the tender flesh above the bull's upper lip, and the bull bellowed in pain and rage as it tried to shake the great dog loose.

Michael began to scream as a shower of warm blood and saliva reached his face and arms. He backed up, stumbled, and was buried beneath the dead weight of the dog. Boy and beast regained their feet, the dog keeping himself between Michael and the bleeding bovine, his barks changing to screaming yelps as the bull tore at him with his horns. Petrified, the boy held his ground, unable to move, his mouth open in a long, silent scream.

"I couldn't be more pleased." Teresa Dundee held the heavy silver hairbrush in her hand, her long fingers tracing the gold-filled monogram on its back. She lifted her head and was rewarded with a tender kiss from Angela.

Everyone heard the boy's scream then, his cry one with the angry, pained yelps of the dog. No one said a word as en masse they rose from their chairs, bumping shoulders as they raced through the door. Estevan saw the great cloud of dust and debris above the corral, and knowing there would be a need, he grabbed for the rifle that hung beside the door and levered a shell into the chamber.

Cooper reached the enclosure before the others, the sound of his heart growing louder, more intense, as he spied the boy. Without thinking, he dove through the fence, landing hard and rolling over before he found his feet. He made a frantic grab for the boy, dropping to the ground, Michael warm and fragile beneath him, as the bull made another pass. Cooper covered his head with his arm and felt a tingling sensation of hoof against bone as his elbow was jarred by a quick blow that sent fire down the long bone to his fingertips. He felt his gorge rise and clenched his teeth against the sickness, using numb fingers to push himself to his knees and then to his feet. With the boy tucked safely under his arm, he sprinted toward the gate. There was a loud explosion, close to his ear, and then the gentle, faraway *oof* as the slug ripped into the bull's head and the beast collapsed at his heels.

Cooper stood there for a time, winded, the boy clutched to his chest. Fear gave way to anger, and he held the child up, unable to speak. He was relieved when Regan pried the boy away from his fingers.

Her inspection was quick and thorough, her face white as she poked and probed at Michael's arms and legs. He pulled away from her, angry at her show of concern, no longer afraid—now that the danger had passed. "I'm all right, Regan," he pouted. "Dammit. I'm all right!"

The woman slowly stood up, the color gradually returning to her face. Feeling Teresa at her side, she turned, her eyes speaking more effectively than her tongue. Teresa nodded and pressed something into Regan's hand.

Instinctively, Regan's fingers curled around the object. Then she looked down, smiling with understanding as she recognized the large, flat-backed silver hairbrush that Angela had given her mother. "Michael," she breathed.

The spanking was quick, public, and properly painful. The humiliation burned more deeply than the actual blows, and the boy's chin trembled as he tried hard not to cry. "I hate you," he yelled, his voice rising. "I hate you!" He turned and ran, disappearing into the comforting quiet and blackness beyond the barn door.

Devastated, Regan started to follow after him, but she felt a sudden pressure of strong fingers on the soft flesh of her upper arm, and she pulled up short. "Let him go," Cooper urged. When she started to protest, he shook his head. "He'll be fine," he said gently. Then Jonathan was beside them, and he took Regan's free arm. Cooper let go and left, trailing after the boy and the dog.

He found them in the hayloft, the boy's head buried in the black thickness of the dog's neck. Silently, he eased himself into the softness of the piled hay, content to wait. The smile came then, as he remembered his own childhood and the many times that he had hidden himself away to cry and curse the unfairness of his punishment while he sought to soothe away the dual torment of his tender backside and bruised feelings. He picked up a piece of straw and began chewing.

"She was right, you know," he said softly. The boy's sobs stopped, and Cooper reached out to scratch the dog's ear. Michael's fingers closed around his hand and held him. "You were told to stay away from the pens, boy," he scolded. "You deserved what you got, Michael. If Regan hadn't paddled your butt, I would have."

Michael sniffled, and Cooper gave him his handkerchief. Tiny specks of dust and chaff danced in the air about his head when he blew his nose. Handing back the damp cloth, the boy asked, "Would you have spanked me hard, too?"

Cooper ignored the quavering, theatrical sobs. "Damned hard," he answered truthfully.

Teresa waited until the others had retired and the house was quiet before she sought out her son. "We need to talk, Cooper."

He didn't answer. The glow of his cigarette marked a precise path as he raised and lowered the smoke to and from his mouth. There was a long pause as he pinched the short stub between his thumb and forefinger and inhaled for the last time, the tip of the cigarette a bright, cherry red. Although the darkness hid the grim tightness of his features, the quiet anger was obvious in the stubborn set of his jaw and the near whisper of his words. "There isn't anything to talk about, Teresa. You've already made up your mind."

Teresa—he always calls me Teresa when he is angry with me, she thought. "I want you to listen to me, Cooper. Jonathan—"

"Jonathan doesn't give a damn about anything but Jonathan!" There was the soft sound of tissue fluttering in the night breeze as he began rolling another cigarette. The anger made it an impossible job, and he swore, crumpling up the paper and tobacco and flipping it onto the patio floor.

Teresa moved closer to her son, her hand massaging the tense muscle in his upper arm. "I've seen Regan's reports, Cooper. And I've listened to everything—*everything*—that Jonathan had to say."

He rolled his shoulders, fighting the fatigue, remembering

the long discussion between Jonathan and Teresa as they finished the last of the dinner wine. He'd never seen that kind of rapport between his half brother and his mother, and it hurt. "I didn't think that you'd side with him. Not in this."

She laughed gently and muffled the sound with her hand. "You sound like you're ten years old and I've just taken away your favorite toy because you refused to share!" She shook her head, kneading his arm with her fingers. "The line has been losing money for almost a year, Cooper." Her voice had changed, her tone officious and businesslike. "Whether it's luck or bad planning, the losses are getting worse. Not just the monetary losses, but also the losses we've taken in damaged equipment, injured livestock. It's got to stop, Cooper. Even Malachai would have agreed that it has to stop."

The mention of his father's name brought with it an old rage and an old conviction. "Malachai didn't die in an accident," he murmured stubbornly, knowing that she still believed otherwise. He faced his mother. "Just give me a month. Get Jonathan to give me a month! No interference, no arguments, no hassles about how I choose to stop what's been happening." He was pleading with her. "A month," he repeated.

She shook her head, disappointed that he didn't understand, her heart filled with the same terrible fear and grief that had almost crippled her when Malachai died. Losing her husband had been bad enough. Almost losing her son had been even worse.

The grief had consumed Coop. For a long time after Malachai's death, he retreated into himself, looking for someone to blame, someone to vent his anger and rage on as he drank himself into a silent, impenetrable shell. "It's time to let go, Cooper," she whispered, burying her head against his chest. "You've got to let go. . . ."

She was crying. He could feel her tears against his shirt, the warmth stinging against his skin and quickly growing cold. He said nothing, holding her close, truly sorry for her hurt and pain. He was even more sorry that he could not bring himself to stop it.

Chapter 8

Delgado's men were hidden in the scrub beyond the hacienda, well concealed by a thick cover of mesquite and tumbleweed. They had been there for over two hours, arriving just after sunset. Ramón Delgado watched through a telescope; the house was completely dark and everything was quiet, with the unnatural stillness that came in the ebony blackness of a desert night.

Logan Montgomery was with the gang of marauders, a surprising visitor in a place where he clearly did not belong. Already the speculator's mood had deteriorated beyond the point of polite control, and his words were bitter, curt. "I don't want anything to happen to Jonathan Dundee," he growled, not really giving a damn about the man himself. "I'll need him after this is over. At least for a while."

Delgado kicked out at one of his men, knocking a cigarillo from the man's hand before he could light it. "What about the girl?" he asked. He smiled across at Montgomery, choosing this method to tell the man that Angela Dundee was also in the house.

"The girl?" Montgomery echoed.

Delgado took a drink from the jug he had been hoarding. "I sent Breed ahead to watch the house," he explained. "Angela Dundee was on the stage when they came in from Casa Grande," he said hoarsely. "Jonathan came later, after the rodeo." He smiled, thinking of the two young women. His smile grew as he anticipated the diversion they would provide when he took them.

Montgomery interrupted his dark musings. "I don't give a damn about the girl," he said finally, working the thing over in his mind. "Jonathan is the key. I'll need Jonathan just long enough to expedite a sale," he breathed. "And make sure at least some of the legislators are left alive."

Delgado hid his smile behind the bottle. He finished the drink, rolling the jug between his palms. "Are you staying for the festivities?" he asked.

Montgomery shook his head. He stared into the predawn darkness, his eyes probing the figures that huddled among the brush, the thick clumps of tumbleweed. "You know better, Ramón." He punched the man's arm, smiling. "I leave it all in your able hands," he said magnanimously.

He took his leave then, picking his way cautiously through the maze of scrub and mute men to the place where his buggy and driver were waiting, and then he was gone.

Delgado listened to the fading noise of gravel and sand as the buggy rolled away from the campsite. His hand flexed, and he wiggled his fingers at Breed Tatum, signaling for yet another bottle.

Tatum came over, surrendered the jug, and stood there, flailing his arms in a futile attempt to warm himself. White vapor preceded his words. "I could use a fire, *jefe*," he complained.

Delgado lifted the bottle, shaking it and letting the potent mescal slosh against the sides. "This is all the fire you need," he laughed. "All the fire any of us will need."

They passed the remaining hours until dawn drinking and applying the vegetable tannins needed to dye their skin the proper shades of bronze. As the morning wore on, the serapes and muslin shirts gave way to bare chests and leather leggings. Brightly colored headbands tamed hair that was now parted in the middle, and appropriate beadwork and amulets hung from their necks.

Delgado was a thorough and experienced organizer. In the past, he had utilized his special talents in many ways, just as he had led many similar raids. Priding himself on his successful ruses, he examined each man personally, adjusting a headband here, applying a measure more of dye there. In the end, they were perfect duplicates of the Apache warriors they would soon imitate.

And then he waited, patiently anticipating the kill.

Cooper swore, the loud clatter of metal against metal shattering the early morning stillness. He worked the grid back into place on the stove, almost burning his fingers, and set about making a proper pot of coffee.

"You always up before the birds, Coop?" Estevan stifled a yawn, the sarcasm adding a sharp edge to his voice.

"Couldn't sleep," the other answered truthfully. He stretched, trying to ease the sore ache in his back, and heard the dry crack of bone as his joints rebelled.

"We've got almost two hours before we're due to leave," Estevan groused. He stared at the enamel coffeepot, wondering if it was true, the old homily about watched pots. "I could handle something a little stronger—and quicker—Coop," he said finally, pointing at the stove.

Cooper nodded. He rummaged around on the shelf above the sink, his hand finally closing around a bottle of vintage brandy. The aroma of coffee began to rise as the pot started to boil, and he hesitated, as if waiting for his friend to change his mind.

Estevan shoved two mugs across the counter. "We can always mix it," he grinned.

"Not in my house—and not this early in the morning!" Teresa Dundee joined them, the hem of her skirt sweeping the floor as she crossed the kitchen. As Estevan reached for the brandy, she smacked at his hand with a large wooden spoon, laughing when he pulled away. "After you've eaten," she promised, relenting.

She passed in front of Cooper, pausing when he reached out and pulled her close in a quick hug. The tenseness was still there, and she knew that nothing had been resolved, but it made his kiss no less sweet. "Ham and eggs?" she smiled.

Cooper rubbed his belly. "And biscuits," he teased. "At least a dozen of them!" He knew that she had already started the sourdough, for a thin dusting of flour covered her apron.

Around them, the house came alive. Aaron Beitermann entered the kitchen, yawning and scratching as he followed his nose to the good smells. He helped himself to the coffee, swearing softly when he burned his hand on the handle, grateful when Teresa handed him a pad. The others came after him, each of them fully dressed, huddling around the stove for their share of early morning warmth.

Jonathan was the last to come into the room. He waited as Angela filled his mug, and then took his place at the head of the table. Regan was on his right, and he reached over to briefly touch her hand. His words, however, were directed at Cooper. "Looks like we could get an early start," he smiled.

Cooper felt his mother's eyes on him and answered his brother accordingly. "Are you making the rest of the ride with us?"

"I've been considering it," Jonathan answered. He blew into his cup, watching Cooper intently.

The smile failed to reach Cooper's eyes. "Partner's privilege," Cooper commented. He was finding it more and more difficult to remain civil. "It'll give us a chance to talk, big brother—once we get to Tucson." He wanted Jonathan to know he was still opposed to the sale, that Teresa had not convinced him that it would be right to sell—that nothing in this world or the next would convince him it was necessary to sell.

Jonathan was aware of a gentle pressure on his hand. He could feel Regan's fingers flexing across his knuckles, and he

returned the caress. Teresa's eyes were on him as well, and
out of respect—if not an awakening affection—he held his
temper. "We can talk anytime, Coop. I've never once refused to talk."

"I want you to *listen* this time, Jonathan," Cooper breathed.
There was an awkward silence as the two brothers exchanged
a long look.

"Your eggs, Coop," Teresa said softly. She handed the
man his plate and nodded at his chair.

The morning meal progressed with an air of normalcy,
Angela's presence tempering even the most corrosive of moods.
She hovered over her small family, dividing her time between
Jonathan and Cooper, somehow reserving enough time to
help Teresa with the serving and still able to joke with
Michael and Estevan.

Coop rose and excused himself, still laughing at the steady
exchange between Estevan and Angela. "You ought to marry
her, *compadre*," he teased. "Then when she gets out of
line, you can swat her!"

Angela took a swing at her brother, laughing as he danced
away. "He'd never find a big enough club, fool! Besides
which," she bragged, patting her own chest, "he knows that
I'm a better shot than he is—something you'd both better
keep in mind," she warned.

Estevan raised his hands in a gesture of submission. Rising
from his chair and stuffing the last bit of ham into his mouth,
he reached out, grabbing hold of the young woman's sleeves.
"You're in dire need of a good lesson in manners, and the
proper measure of respect for your elders!" He kissed her on
the mouth, then followed Cooper through the open door.

They walked across the dusty compound and entered the
stock barn shoulder to shoulder, pausing at the sill to allow
their eyes to adjust to the darkness. Coop heard the gentle
whoof as one of the coach horses snorted in greeting, and
then the subtle rustle of hay as another rose up from the straw

bedding. "Fat and sassy," Cooper smiled, leading the way to the stalls. "A couple of days at the home ranch and they get lazy as hell."

Estevan stumbled over a clump of matted straw. "You treat them like babies, Coop. Grain-fed, spoiled babies."

Cooper was inside the first stall, haltering the big black gelding that was his favorite. He led the horse out into the corridor, using his fingers to flick off the bits of straw that clung to the horse's dark hide. "Good care, good service," he declared. "If Malachai taught me anything, he taught me that." He ground-reined the animal and grabbed Estevan's arm. "I want you to see this," he said proudly, leading the way.

The barn was immense. The structure had been built the year following the end of the Civil War, when Malachai Dundee sold horses as remounts for the rapidly growing cavalry that populated the forts throughout the territory. Large consignments of stock, bred for endurance and speed, had passed through this barn, sturdy little bay mounts sired by the Morgan stud Malachai had imported from the East to mate with his mixed-blood Spanish and mustang mares. The Morgan stud bred true, passing his even temperament and coloring to his colts. His progeny pulled the wagons, drove the cows, and carried cattleman and soldier alike as the Anglos flooded into the territory. They were beautiful animals, known for their endurance and their longevity, and Cooper and Teresa had continued the line.

Cooper led Estevan into the back corridor. He gestured with an outstretched arm, making a sweeping arc that encompassed both sides of the wide aisle.

"Damn," Estevan breathed. His eyes lit up with the same peculiar fire that warmed Cooper's, a horseman's appreciation for perfect conformation. His gaze shifted from stall to stall; the animals were magnificent, all twenty of them. Estevan felt as though he were standing in a great hall of mirrors, as if he were seeing one horse reflected twenty times in a long corridor of silvered glass. "My God, Coop."

Cooper laughed. "Malachai's one great passion," he said proudly. "Or his most expensive vice, if you consider what it cost him." He moved down the corridor, knowing that Estevan was behind him. Nodding at the stalls, Cooper continued, "Five years and a hundred mares, and this is what he kept. . . ."

Estevan was inside one of the stalls, his hands moving lightly across a yearling filly's neck and forelegs. He lifted one leg, marveling again at the fine conformation. "I thought Malachai had given up the horse business a long time ago," he thought aloud. He wiped the palms of his hands together, careful to relatch the stall gate as he came through.

Cooper looped an arm around the man's shoulders, leading the way back to the front of the barn. He smiled. "My mother wanted him to have something to keep him busy when the day came—" he cleared his throat "—when the day came that he had to quit working the line."

"I'd have been his first customer." Estevan's mind was still filled with the memory of the filly and the others. He scratched at the day-old beard shadowing his chin. "I'll be *your* first customer," he promised.

Cooper shook his head. "I haven't given up working the line," he answered.

Wisely, Estevan let it drop. He remained silent, helping as Coop harnessed the six coach horses, his fingers nimbly working the leather and buckles. Together, they led the animals out of the barn and into the yard.

From his vantage point beyond the house, Delgado watched as Coop and Estevan led the dray horses into place in front of the coach. Smiling, he stripped off the serape that he wore over a faded government-issue shirt. His own headband was in place, and at his waist he wore a well-used cartridge belt, the tarnished brass insignia dull and grimy from constant use.

A knife scabbard hung in easy reach at the small of his back, and he fingered the haft absently.

"Now?" Tatum asked, pressing close to the man's shoulder.

"Not yet," Delgado cautioned. "Not until the coach is loaded and on its way. Divide and conquer," he mused smugly. "Separate the coach from the house—from the people and the arms within the house."

Teresa stood on the tiled veranda where she made her brief good-byes, knowing that in all likelihood this would be the last time Aaron Beitermann and his fellow legislators would make this trip. It was more than the sale of the stage line that would stop it; it was the subtle differences she had sensed this time, just as she had sensed the growing restlessness and uneasiness that the men displayed when they were not being entertained. *I'm sorry, Malachai,* she thought. Somehow, she felt she had failed the man, failed his memory.

"They're ready to leave, Mother." Angela read the look in Teresa's eyes and felt sad for her. Her own smile did little to comfort the woman.

"Jonathan's going to go with them, isn't he?" Teresa took one of Angela's hands in both of her own. *God help her,* she mused silently. *She loves him; she really loves him.*

"He wants to spend some time with Regan," Angela finally answered. "And who can blame him?" She shrugged, keeping hold of Teresa's hand as they went out into the yard. "She'll make him a good wife, Mama. A proper wife . . ."

Michael was waiting for them. He gave Teresa a broad smile as she stuffed a wrapped package of sweets into one of his pockets and filled the other with a similar packet of dried meat for the dog. She bent down, until her eyes were level with the child's, and put one hand on each arm. "If my sons had been more diligent, Michael," she smiled, "I'd have a grandchild just about your age! And I'd give him a hug, not a handshake." She swept the boy into her arms and held him for a long time.

Coop had already coaxed the dog aboard. He lifted Michael away from Teresa, his hand lingering on the woman's cheek. He directed his words at the boy, but meant for Teresa to hear them. "That's *my* mama your stealing kisses from, little man. And I'm not so sure I want to share." He kissed her then and was warmed by her smile.

There was a thump behind him as Jonathan tossed the government pay satchel back into the luggage boot, and then a flurry of hugs as Angela, Regan, and Teresa said their farewells. Awkwardly, Jonathan took Teresa's hand and pulled her close in a quick, embarrassed hug. He helped Regan into the coach and then followed her aboard, sticking his head out to call to his brother, "All loaded."

Nodding his head, Cooper bent down and held his arms out for Michael. He hoisted the boy up onto the driver's seat, using a hand on the boy's rump to boost him aboard.

Suddenly, a single shot rang out, thundering across the yard and shattering the calm. Instinctively, Cooper flattened himself against the ground. He looked up and was grateful that Estevan had had the presence of mind to drag the youngster down to a place of relative safety behind the front wheel. Cooper then stood and reached up into the boot, his fingers closing around the payroll satchel. He ran around to the other side. "In the house!" he bellowed. "Everyone in the house!"

Delgado leaped up from his place behind a clump of scrub brush and screamed in rage, furious that someone had fired before being given the signal. He turned and strode around in a circle as he surveyed his men. Breed Tatum and Benito Chavez—one on either side of him—made the same circle, their eyes predatory. They found their man, the mercenary's weapon still smoking. He backed away drunkenly, his legs rubber beneath him, his laughter rising to a hysterical pitch as Delgado and Tatum moved toward him.

Delgado swore. "Fool! You goddamn fool!" His hand disappeared behind his back, reappearing surprisingly fast, the flash of steel seeming to shoot from his fingertips. The knife blade sliced through fabric and skin to find its resting place directly beneath the man's sternum. The blow knocked the man backward, and he grabbed at the haft, pulling the knife free in the final surge of will that was left within him. Blood poured from the wound, bright red against the faded shirt. His mouth opened wide, no words coming, and he dropped to his knees. He held the knife out, as if offering Delgado a gift, and fell face forward into the dirt.

The bandit chief picked up the knife, wiping the blade on the dead man's shirt. "Now!" he ordered. "Now!" Around him, the men came alive. Tatum's voice lifted in a shrill war whoop, and the raiders mounted and fell in behind him as he made the first charge.

Cooper was the last person into the house, the big dog at his heels. He came into the room directly behind Orrin Pryor, shielding the man with his own body as they came through the door. There was no hesitation in him. He tossed the canvas pay satchel into the far corner, his back pressed against the door as he slammed it shut.

Jonathan and Estevan were immediately beside him. He pulled a heavy four-inch-thick plank from the alcove beside the main door, grimacing as he lifted it into place. It took all three men to work the iron-bound bar into the heavy brackets that extended chest high from the wall on either side of the door. Finished, they backed away, exchanging startled glances as the first of a series of bullets tore into the heavy door. "Jesus Christ, Coop," Jonathan exclaimed. "What the hell is going on?"

"Apaches!" Aaron Beitermann shouted from his position at a narrow gunport on the far wall. He pointed at the small opening, as if the others could see outside, and repeated the word. Vehemently. "*Apaches!*"

Angela screamed. She backed against the table, her hand pressed against her mouth, the old terror coming back. Teresa rushed to her side, pulling her hands away from her face, "No!" she said firmly. "They are not Apache. We would never be attacked by the Apache!"

The house was a virtual fortress, the adobe walls three feet thick. The windows had already been barred and shuttered from within, leaving as the only openings the narrow gunports— slits—that were staggered in lines of threes. It was the same on all four outer walls.

Beitermann, Pryor, Moorhouse, and Kilmont were in a cluster in the opposite corner. They shared a hurried and hushed conversation, stopping only long enough to call for Jonathan. Estevan and Cooper were immediately aware of their exclusion, but they shrugged it off, knowing there was no time to indulge in the petty prejudices the other men were no longer able to control. Methodically, they removed the assortment of firearms from the gun cabinets in Malachai's old office, passing them hand to hand with Regan, Teresa, and Angela to the main room.

Estevan chose a Henry repeating rifle. As he stood feeding shells into the chamber, he was relieved at the workings of the well-oiled mechanism. Someone had taken great care to preserve the rifle, to keep it in good working condition— someone who knew what he was doing. He felt Cooper's eyes on him and lifted the gun, balancing it in the flat of his hand. "Is this what you were doing when you weren't able to sleep last night?" he asked quietly.

"Old habit," Cooper answered. "My once-a-year chore when I come home." He stared across at his friend. "I didn't think we'd ever have to use them, *compadre*."

"Did I ask you that?" the other retorted. He canted the rifle against his shoulder. "And now?"

"We arm your esteemed colleagues," Cooper answered. He stared at the shaft of sunlight that poured through a gunport on the front wall, marking its angle as it hit the tiled floor. "Going to be a long day, Estevan—a long, hot day."

Chapter 9

A sullen silence hung over the room, the sudden lull in the fighting heightening the tensions within the house. The four older legislators remained segregated, manning adjacent gunports, their shared conversations hushed and secretive. Now and then they cast a covert look at Teresa or Angela, their faces plainly showing the feelings of hostility that were now resurfacing and finding new direction.

Aaron Beitermann's hatred ran deepest. He had spent forty years in the territory and had lost two families in the blood-baths that occurred with frightening regularity in the early years. Two wives, four sons, and two infant daughters. He had lost all but his youngest son to the Apache.

Orrin Pryor and Jarrod Kilmont had had losses that were less devastating, but which equally marked the men. They had each lost a brother to Cochise and the Chiracahuas in the early '60s, and the pain of those losses was still with them.

Lester Moorhouse's motives—his hatreds—were financially inspired. He coveted the land and could find no good reason for the government to support a people who contributed nothing to the growth of the territory or to its anticipated statehood. He firmly believed that the only good Indian was a dead Indian. And he was vehemently against assimilation by miscegenation.

Together, the four men nursed their bitterness, blaming the

Apache for their past injuries and their present difficulties. The Dundees, because of their Indian blood, bore the brunt of that bitterness.

Beitermann was the first to voice his feelings. He stood with his back to the women, declaring loudly to his comrades, "We're going to die here." He kicked at the pile of spent shell casings that lay in a ragged pile at his feet. "Goddamned if we aren't going to die here. . . ."

Cooper shoved himself away from the wall. He had used the hiatus to reload his Winchester and catnap, but he was wide awake now, keenly aware of the tension that filled the room—just as he was sharply aware of the increased hostility directed toward his mother and his sister. He joined the two women, doing his best to divert their attention, forcing a calm and a humor he didn't feel. He smacked Angela on the rump, grabbing her hand when she tried to retaliate. "Man could starve to death around here long before he'd get shot," he grinned. He tapped the thick wall with the barrel of his rifle to emphasize his point.

Teresa knew that he spoke the truth. Still, there were other things that concerned the woman. She tugged at Angela's sleeve. "Ask Regan if she'll help you, darling." Her gaze shifted to the other woman, then to the boy. "And Michael," she whispered. "Keep them busy." She waited until Angela was gone before she spoke again. "Coop, if this goes on too long, we're going to run out of water."

The siege resumed suddenly, without warning; the roar of man-made thunder rolled across the desert floor as the mercenaries unleashed a steady barrage of rifle fire. The interior of the room filled with an acrid blue smoke as Jonathan and the others fired in return. The dull thud of bullets hitting the adobe was punctuated by the high-pitched whine of lead ricocheting off the metal hinges and hardware on the front door. Instinctively, the men at the gunports ducked and pulled away.

Michael entered the room carrying a plate of hastily made

sandwiches just as a bullet whistled through the untended gunport above his head. The slug smashed into the clay *botilla* hanging suspended from the heavy rafters, the earthenware pot shattering as the lead exited on the opposite side. The tepid water showered down on the boy, drenching his hair and face. It was a terrifying moment for the child, the warm water feeling like blood, and he began to scream. The heavy platter of food tumbled from his hands to the floor, shattering against the smooth tile.

Teresa responded to the boy's cries. She swept him off his feet, carrying him across the room to a safe corner between Beitermann and Jonathan. She dried his hair with her apron, showing him there was no blood on the wet cloth. "It's all right, Michael. Everything is going to be all right," she crooned.

Bravely, the boy held back his tears. "But Indians . . ." he whispered. He held tightly to the woman's fingers, his eyes begging for more comfort.

"They're not Indians, Michael," she answered.

It was more than Beitermann could stand. He hunkered down, his fingers grabbing for Teresa's arm. Roughly, oblivious of the boy, he shook her. "Take a look," he ordered, pulling her to her feet. "Dammit! Take a look!" He shoved her against the rough-surfaced wall, using his free hand to press her face flush with the narrow opening. "Tell me *now* that they aren't Apache!" he hissed.

"Take your hands off her, Aaron."

The words came from between clenched teeth. Cooper's jaw was tight, his lips a narrow, dark line, and they barely moved when he repeated the words. "Take your hands off her, Aaron. *Now!*"

Beitermann half turned, his hand still closed around the nape of the woman's neck. "Tell the boy what you see, woman," he seethed. He held her in place, moving so that his body was between Cooper and Teresa. "Tell him!"

A bullet tore into the window shutter just above Teresa's

forehead, and she knew the very real terror of sudden death. The wood splintered, and she shut her eyes against the shower of slivers. Still, she did not answer.

The curse came from the depths of Cooper's belly, roaring up deep from within. "You *bastard*!" Using the butt of his rifle, he struck out at Beitermann's belly, jamming the stock into the thick layer of fat above the man's belt. Letting Beitermann collapse, he dropped the rifle and began hammering viciously at the man's face with his fists.

"Stop it!" Estevan grabbed at Cooper's shoulders. Jonathan moved behind Beitermann and grasped the loose fabric at the back of his neck. He pulled the man away from Cooper's hands, stunned by the naked fury he saw in his brother's face.

Estevan's forearm was pressed against Cooper's windpipe, and he increased the pressure of his hold, forcing Cooper backward as he pulled him away. He held him for a long time, feeling the stiffness and anger beneath his fingers, the whole time watching Jonathan's eyes for some sign that it was all right to let go. It seemed that hours passed before the elder Dundee finally nodded his head. Cautiously, Estevan relaxed his hold.

The suddenness of Beitermann's attack on the woman, and Cooper's response, had caught them all unaware. One by one, the others turned away from their places at the gunports, their weapons silent. Estevan sensed the strained quiet, and used it. "This has got to stop," he said finally. He moved in front of Cooper, addressing the others as well. "This has become a house divided," he began, paraphrasing Lincoln. "If we're going to get out of here—if we're going to survive this and walk away—we've got to work together. All of us," he declared. He lifted his hand when Beitermann started to protest. "*All* of us," he repeated.

"Then tell the woman to shut up," Pryor spoke up from his place at the back wall.

Kilmont echoed the man's complaints. "Yeah, we're all

getting tired of hearing it, Folley. Of hearing her say that those—'' he pointed with the barrel of his gun to someplace far beyond the house ''—aren't Apache.''

Teresa dabbed at her forehead. A freckling of dried blood was above her eye, but she impatiently waved Cooper away when he tried to tend her. "I'm aware of your feelings, Mr. Pryor," she began softly. Her eyes shifted from one legislator to the other in turn, finally settling on Beitermann. "And yours, Aaron."

She sighed. "Not once in all the years I've been here has there been an Apache who came to the place to do anyone—'' she stressed the word ''—*anyone* any harm.'' She smiled suddenly, to the surprise of the others. "Why do you think Malachai brought me here, Aaron?" She was speaking now in terms he would understand—terms that bespoke of treaties and secret agreements. "Why do you think he took me as his wife? Because, Aaron, I brought peace to this house as my dowry."

Beitermann refused to be swayed. He eyed the woman through narrowed lids, like a snake attempting to mesmerize his morning meal. "Malachai isn't here, woman. He may have made treaties with them, but it was this—'' he held up his rifle ''—Malachai's willingness to use this—that kept them away.''

Sadly, Teresa shook her head. "I don't give a damn what you think, Aaron—what any of you think. We are not fighting the Apache!" A renewed volley of rifle fire convinced them all that she was lying.

The long morning dragged on, the nerve-wracking ceremony of long periods of quiet and long periods of intense fire tearing at the ragged edges of their joint sanity. The house—which had been their haven, their fortress—was now their prison. It would soon be their tomb.

Estevan joined Cooper at his position, a scattering of brass shell casings rolling away from his feet as he moved across the room. He signaled for Jonathan to join them, watching as

Regan took the man's place at the gunport. Then Teresa moved in to cover Cooper's place, just as Angela had taken Estevan's, and the men moved away to a private corner of the room. Estevan whispered, "We've got to get some help, Coop. We've got to get someone out of here and over to Fort Lowell." He toed the empty cartridges that lay in bright profusion at his feet.

Jonathan hunkered down, his arms resting easily on his thighs, his fingers busy. Cooper joined him, sitting back on his heels, their sibling animosities no longer important. Estevan chose to sit on the floor, his tired back and shoulders resting against the cold wall. Cooper was the first to speak. "You're right, Estevan," he breathed. "You and I can make the ride."

Jonathan interrupted him as Cooper was about to continue. The elder Dundee's face was grim, his eyes on Teresa. "I will go with Estevan," he corrected. He touched Cooper's knee with one finger, emphasizing his words. He nodded at Teresa, and then at Angela. "I think that it's important that you be here for them." He did not put his fears into words, knowing that Cooper—when he thought about it—would understand. When that understanding seemed slow in coming, he spoke again. "I don't think I could stop Beitermann if he started again." He wasn't speaking of a physical weakness now. "He isn't afraid of me, Coop. Nor the others. They aren't afraid of what I might do if Aaron starts on Teresa again."

"And they are afraid of me?" Cooper asked. The words were as dry as his throat.

"They have reason to be afraid of you, Coop," Estevan answered the question, his voice secretive. "Of your temper. Your vindictiveness." He was remembering the reaction of the legislators when Cooper took on the man at the way station.

Cooper nodded. It was true. As long as he kept them more afraid of him than they were of the men outside, he could keep them in line—keep them fighting. "You'll have to wait until it gets dark," he breathed. "You can get into the barn, get to the horses." He looked up at his brother. "You'll have to make the ride bareback, with a second horse in tow for a remount."

Jonathan nodded. Already, his backside was burning. "I can make the ride, Coop." He smiled a wry smile, thinking of another, more real danger. "If I don't get shot," he reasoned.

Cooper's grin crinkled the skin around his eyes. "You do make a fine target, Jonathan," he joshed. "A lot bigger than Estevan."

"Sure," Jonathan answered. "Send me out as your decoy. That's the whole idea behind two of us making the break, isn't it?" He took a playful swing at his brother's head. "When I get to heaven, I'll just tell Malachai it was all your fault; then *you* can spend eternity trying to convince him it was not!"

"You ain't going to heaven," Cooper laughed. "You've been a lawyer too many years to go anywhere but straight to hell!" His mood changed, and he grew serious. "You two'll be all right. New moon tonight, and there won't be much light. You'll be just fine. . . ."

The gunfire resumed, and all three men flinched. It was worse now. Each time after the long quiet, the effect of the renewed gunfire was worse. It jarred their senses, electrifying raw nerves just below the surface, giving them the feeling that they were going to jump out of their skins and expose their naked fears to the world. Jonathan wiped a shaking hand across his upper lip. "At least we have the horses," he breathed, feeling a need to hear his own voice and those particular words.

Cooper stood up, heading back toward his gunport. He stopped just long enough to reply. "Think about that, Jonathan. If that is the Apache out there," he nodded toward the windows, "then why do we still have the horses?"

Jonathan's mouth dropped open. His brow furrowed as he considered his brother's words, an insidious doubt beginning to gnaw at his belly. *Why do we have the horses?* If this had been a raid to gain wealth, the Apache would have hit and run, stampeding the stock in the corrals and cutting loose the livestock inside the barn. They would have taken the animals and run.

And if this was an attack on the house—on the people within the house—then the horses wouldn't have mattered. The Apache would have slaughtered the animals and set fire to the barns and the house, shooting everyone foolish enough to flee the flames.

Logan Montgomery and Ramón Delgado. The images of the two men rose up specterlike before Jonathan's eyes. He screwed his eyes shut, shaking his head. *No,* he thought. *No!*

Delgado knew the frustration of a man whose plans had been torn away by the stupidity of one person's rash act. The early shot had robbed him of his anticipated advantage, and what should have been an easy foray against two separate targets was now a major assault against a single well-fortified objective.

He knew the house well. As a boy—when his father was fool enough to work for the man who had stolen his birthright—he often had been inside the house. Even then, he had felt the invulnerability of the place, the safety behind the thick clay walls.

The house had been built in the shape of a square. The back side of the structure opened on a broad expanse of cleared land that made an attack from the rear virtually impossible. The two adjacent arms of the square faced each other across a covered patio that led to the main room of the house. This room ran the entire length of the fourth side of the square.

Thus, the well-barricaded house provided those inside its walls a sweeping view of the terrain—front, sides, and back.

Properly armed, the defenders inside the house could hold an army at bay for days, weeks. And they were well armed. Delgado remembered Malachai Dundee's passion for preparedness. An arsenal lay beyond the heavy, iron-bound doors—a wealth of guns and ammunition.

Benito Chavez understood Delgado's pensive silence. With Breed Tatum, he stood at Delgado's back, waiting for their leader to move. It was a short wait. "We're going to fire the barn." Delgado was accustomed to thinking on his feet. "We're going to pull the men out of the house—*away* from the house."

Tatum nodded. "What about the coach?" he asked. Chavez echoed the question.

Delgado answered without any hesitation. "They'll try to use it for cover when they make a break for the barn," he thought aloud. The smile crawled across his face, exposing the man's teeth. "Kill the horses," he ordered. "Shoot them where they stand." No horses, no way to move the coach—and no cover.

He reached out, taking the long-barreled, single-shot Sharps that Chavez preferred to the repeating rifles favored by the others. The old gun had a range in excess of a thousand yards. Delgado pressed the stock against his shoulder, cocked the piece, and fired.

Jonathan was watching out the gunport as the first horse fell. The big gelding's dark head turned a brilliant red, a hole the size of a man's fist opening beneath his ear. Then the animal collapsed, disappearing behind its harness mate as it fell to the ground in a tangle of metal and leather. With cruel regularity the other five frantic horses followed.

Enraged, Jonathan levered off seven rounds in quick succession, firing at targets he couldn't see. "Still think it's not the Apache, Coop?" He shouted the words, almost relieved that the raiders *were* Indians and not Montgomery's henchmen. "Still think so now?"

Estevan answered before Cooper had a chance. "Doesn't make a damn who they are," he declared. He pivoted at his slit, following a bobbing figure that was sprinting toward the barn. "They're going to fire the barn!" he roared. "Goddamn them, they're going to fire the barn!"

More bobbing figures danced across the horizon, bright torches leaving red-orange trailings against the pale-blue sky. Feeling totally helpless, Cooper watched as a billowing black cloud rose up from the barn. He gave himself a single moment of sweet revenge as he picked out his target, satisfaction sweeping him as he saw the man stagger and fall. The torch he had been carrying dropped to the ground and sputtered for a brief moment, about to die out in the sand.

But it was picked up by a second man. The mercenary rolled away from his dead companion, staying close to the ground as he bolted for the barn door. He let out a whoop, disappearing into the darkness of the interior.

The man was gone for a long time. Through the knotholes and gaps in the barn walls, Cooper and the others could see a series of small fires being started on the barn floor. Jointly, the men breathed a silent prayer that went unheard. They watched, united in terror, as the stored hay in the upper loft began to burn.

Chapter 10

The terrified screams of the animals trapped inside the barn reached out to the people confined in the house. Cooper's anguish was plain in his face, his eyes. He stood in, a far corner of the room, apart from all the others, methodically feeding cartridges into a canvas bandolier. A Remington pistol was in place in his holster, a second handgun stuffed inside his belt. His Winchester rifle was rammed beneath his upper arm, the barrel resting on his forearm as he continued loading the cartridge belt. "I'm going out, Jonathan." He spoke to the man without looking at him. "I've got to get to those horses. I'll be back as quickly as I can."

Jonathan nodded his head. Already he was reloading his own rifle. "That smoke is getting pretty thick." He was quiet a moment, reflective, his eyes probing the side wall. "We can go out the window," he said finally.

"No." Angela had joined them. She reached out, her hand closing around Jonathan's arm. Standing beside the two brothers, Estevan saw the move, knowing for certain now that which he had only guessed at before: *Angela was deeply in love with Jonathan.*

Jonathan was not so wise as Estevan. He patted the young woman's cheek, his manner that of an older brother who, although flattered by the attention, did not have the time to listen. "I'll need a cartridge belt, Angela. And so will Estevan."

"Don't go," she pleaded. "Please, Jonathan!" Embarrassed, she stared at the floor. "I don't want any of you to go," she said dully.

Regan had overheard the conversation. She joined them, handing out the cartridge belts Teresa had given her. "Be careful," she warned. Jonathan's hand closed around her own, and she held him. "Please be careful," she said as he slipped away, aware that Angela's eyes were on her.

Covertly, they dropped through the hastily unbarred window—one, then the second, then the third—and there was something final in the way the opening shut behind them. They were now totally on their own. Cooper rested on his heels, his eyes smarting from the smoke. His voice was a hoarse whisper when he declared, "Along there," pointing to a narrow, worn pathway leading off into the thick smoke.

Estevan went first, disappearing into the blue-black haze. Quietly, staying close to the ground, Jonathan followed after him, and he, too, was swallowed up by the darkness.

Inhaling, Cooper traced their steps. He could hear the scratch and roll of loose gravel ahead of him and followed the sound, grateful for the flurry of rifle fire that began to pour from the house. The guns barked singly, then in unison, one rapid round after the other as the legislators and the women provided an effective diversion.

Estevan and Jonathan were waiting at the rear wall of the barn when Cooper broke through the dark vapor. He came up abreast of them, angry that they had not rounded the corner. Estevan pressed his fingers against Cooper's mouth, stopping the words. "We've got company," he whispered. "Two of them, about a hundred yards out, watching the rear door. . . ."

Cooper nodded, immediately understanding their predicament. He contemplated their choices, and then determined what they had to do. Using his hands, he signaled for Estevan and Jonathan to follow his lead, and then, waiting for the gunfire to continue, he began.

Turning the Winchester around in his hands, he began hacking at the rough vertical siding with the rifle stock. Estevan followed suit, the government-issue Henry with its brass butt an even more effective ram. Steadily, he hammered away at the inch-thick panels, timing his blows with the sound of the guns. Jonathan worked with them, the sweat coming profusely at his neck and back as he beat against the boards.

Cooper shouldered his way between Estevan and Jonathan. Sucking in his belly, he ducked and stepped sideways through the narrow opening. Once inside, he resumed pounding, using his feet to kick at the base of the boards, working hard and fast until the opening was wide enough and high enough to suit his needs. And then he disappeared into the barn.

He knew the horses inside the small box stalls as well as he knew himself; his mouth was a tight line as he was forced to make decisions that tore at his heart. The yearlings, the two-year olds, were of no use to him now, and he turned his back on them, forcing his way down the corridor.

He entered the stalls, kicking away the restraining poles. His presence calmed the animals, and they took comfort from his familiar touch, pressing close to him as they followed him out into the corridor. Blindly, they followed after him, the panic subsiding as they felt the cool rush of outside air. Cooper turned, holding the lead horse back. The animal reared up, lifting him off the ground as it tried to break free. Stubbornly—desperately—the man held on, using pressure on the horse's throat and nose to force the gelding's head down. Twisting one ear, he pulled the horse toward the opening and led him through.

Five times, Coop went back into the barn, the smoke becoming more dense, more acrid. Each time, he saw and heard the growing panic of the animals that were still tethered inside their stalls. He watched as the yearling filly Estevan had admired broke loose from her bindings and ran directly into the fire, cursing as her screams reached out to him. The little horse took a long time to die, the stench of burning hair and flesh filling the air before the squeals of pain diminished.

Coop turned his back on the macabre vision and was sick. He emptied his stomach, hating the hell that was all around him, and then ran for the opening.

He had brought out six of the Morgans, although two of the four-year-old animals almost immediately bolted away. He stood, gulping for air, his back pressed against the barn, trying hard to shut his ears to the terrible sounds behind him. "Get them out of here," he coughed, nodding at the horses.

"Coop," Jonathan said, reaching out to his brother, intending to pull him away from the barn. Shaking his head, Cooper knocked the man's arm aside.

He grabbed the Winchester, levering a shell into the chamber. "Go on!" he ordered. "Get out of here!" Knowing what he had to do, he stepped back into the barn. Unable to stop him, Jonathan backed away, following after Estevan. He looked back once and saw Cooper silhouetted against the orange fire.

Systematically, Cooper fired, levered the rifle, and fired again. His stance changed only a little, the rifle moving as he sighted at the more distant targets. One by one, the horses collapsed into the rolling smoke.

From the shelter of rocks beyond the burning barn, Estevan counted: *eleven, twelve, thirteen.* . . The humanlike screams of the horses diminished with each report, until there was nothing—nothing but the roar and crackle of the fire. Estevan wiped the back of his grimy hand across his forehead. "He'll be coming now," he whispered.

Jonathan watched, staring into the smoke. Wraithlike—one leg first, then the barrel of the rifle, and then the whole man—Cooper came out of the haze. His face was covered with black soot, his eyebrows singed, the long trail of his tears starkly white against both cheeks. "My God, Coop," Jonathan breathed.

"I'm all right," the other lied. He pushed his way past his brother, his fingers lingering on Jonathan's sleeve as he passed. He was grateful for the words, the real show of compassion. But the pain was too great now to share with anyone. "We've got to get back to the house," he said finally.

Delgado waited for Tatum's signal. Soon the young renegade rose up from his place of concealment beyond the barn, raising his arm high above his head three times, finishing the gesture with a jabbing point in the direction of the high cluster of rocks midway between the house and the barn.

Satisfied that Cooper and the other two men were now out of action, pinned down among the rocks, Delgado moved. He sprinted across the yard, Chavez and two others right behind him, heading for the fragile, forgotten door to the old part of the house. They jimmied the lock, easing through the opening to the other side. "Through there," Delgado rasped. He led the way—moving swiftly and quietly through the storeroom— past one door, heading directly for another. Pausing, he held a finger up to his lips, gesturing for the others to fall in behind him. Carefully, he tried the doorknob, already knowing that it would be unlocked.

He kicked open the door, charging into the room with his gun drawn, as did the other three right behind him. They did not speak; they just leveled their weapons at the surprised occupants of the main room, making their demands known with a series of coarse grunts. When Delgado finally did speak, the words came in a halting, heavily accented Spanish. *"Los fusiles,"* he croaked. *The guns.*

There was no resistance. Aaron Beitermann and his three associates dropped their rifles and slowly raised their hands, backing against the wall. Chavez sprinted across the room, picking up the discarded weapons. Then, as he covered the four men, his two companions lifted the barricade away from the front door.

Teresa's response was not so cowardly as the men's. Raising up a handgun she had hidden in the folds of her skirt, she took aim.

Tatum slithered through the front door just in time to catch the woman's subtle movement, and he attacked her from behind. His fingers closed around the soft flesh on either side of her neck, the pressure and pain increasing until the pistol fell from her numb fingers. It clattered across the floor to land at Delgado's feet. He kicked it aside.

There was a brief moment of silence as Delgado's eyes filled with a predatory shine. He stepped forward and grabbed Regan's arm. Michael screamed in rage, swearing at the man as he made his charge. Delgado grabbed a handful of the child's thick hair and callously lifted him off his feet and into Chavez's waiting arms.

The dog charged then, coming out of the darkness beneath the table. The low growl became a toothy snarl, and he lunged at Delgado. The Mexican caught him midair, the butt of his rifle smashing against the side of the dog's head. The animal dropped to the floor as if dead, blood pouring from the side of his mouth.

Regan's fury matched the dog's. She broke away from Delgado, raking his face with her long fingernails as she clawed at his eyes and grabbed for Michael. But Chavez tore the boy away from her grasp.

Delgado made a second swing with his rifle, making no attempt to temper the blow, the taste of his own blood fueling the rage in his stomach. The rifle smashed hard against Regan's back, just between the shoulders, the butt of the rifle glancing off the base of her skull. There was a soft, audible sigh as she slipped to the floor, and she lay deathly still beside the dog.

A flurry of gunfire roused the killers into action, and they bolted for the door. Angela was swept from her place beside Teresa, and both women and the boy were carried outside. Then they were gone.

*   *   *

Cooper pressed against the rugged face of the stony hillock, his arm raised in a futile gesture intended to stop the shower of rock that exploded above him. It was a wasted effort, the sharp bits of shale peppering his forearm and unprotected forehead as another bullet ricocheted against the stone pillars.

They were caught in a crossfire, a merciless onslaught that continued without letup as Delgado's henchmen fired on them from two sides. The mercenaries were between the house and the rock cairn where Cooper, Jonathan, and Estevan had taken shelter with the horses. Now a second group of raiders was closing in on them from the flatlands behind the burning barn. It was an effective strategy: The three men were unable to move from the place where they were, and all of them— men and beasts—would soon be cut to ribbons by the terrify- ing hail of ricocheting lead.

Shards of flying stone whistled erractically about their heads, the projectiles as threatening and lethal as the .30 caliber slugs. All three of the men bore the bloody, jagged wounds of the sharp-edged missiles, their forearms and the backs of their ungloved hands speckled with the dried blood of abrasions that opened again and again as they instinctively raised their arms to protect their eyes.

The effect on the string of horses was just as intense. They panicked and began milling about, pressing closer and closer to Cooper, who had taken shelter in a spot below the other two men, separating him from Estevan and Jonathan.

Cooper pulled himself up into the open, scaling the rocks as he attempted to get away from the horses. His exposed leg proved an inviting target, and there was a sharp whine as a bullet skimmed past his knee and splattered on the hard rock. The lead slug split apart on impact, and the larger piece of the bullet slammed into Cooper's exposed thigh well above his knee. It was as if he had been branded with a hot poker and the burning point driven into his leg clear to the bone. Automatically, he grabbed at the wound, his fingers pressing hard to stop the flow of blood. The pain sickened him, and he felt light-headed.

He slipped back down the face of the rock pile, using his rifle as a staff when he landed. There was only occasional gunfire now, the muted pop and crack of handguns more evident than the noise of the long guns. Cooper worked his way among the horses, grateful that the ricochets had ended. Calling out to his two companions, "Try for the house!" he then signaled for Jonathan to toss him his rifle. He yelled the order again. "Take the horses, and make a try for the house! I'll cover you!" he barked.

Jonathan and Estevan needed no further encouragement. Like Cooper, they were aware of the gradual diminishing of hostile fire. Cautiously—placing themselves in the center of the string of horses—the two men made their run.

Cooper stayed behind, laying a blanket of rifle fire in the wake of their retreat, surprised as he watched the raiders disperse and break away. They withdrew into the flatlands beyond the house and smoldering barns, out of range of his rifle, and mounted their horses. But for some reason, they did not run.

Puzzled, Cooper watched as the mounted men bunched up, remaining where they were. They appeared to be watching something—or someone—close to the house. Cooper followed their gaze. He was filled with an unspoken panic when he saw a flash of bright fabric and yellow hair go past his line of vision as five riders sped away from the front of the house, three of the horses carrying a double load. Helpless, he watched as they made their escape, the five mounts swallowed up by the other horses, with the waiting raiders breaking rank to accept them. Together, they thundered off into the desert, disappearing into the scrub beyond the flats.

Cooper made his way back to the house. He limped as he

ran, closing his mind to the pain in his injured thigh, his heart pumping furiously inside a chest that had become too small.

He broke through the back door, stopping himself with both hands and coming to a complete halt before stepping into the room. Jonathan was on his knees beside Regan, gently trying to revive her, one hand cradled tenderly behind her head. Concerned, Cooper eased through the door, grateful when the woman responded to Jonathan's gentle attentions.

A frigid silence greeted him as he crossed the floor. In turn, Beitermann and the other legislators averted their eyes, unable to meet his cold scrutiny. "My mother," he whispered. "Where is my mother?"

Behind him, Regan struggled to sit up. "They took her," she breathed. She swallowed, her eyes probing the shadows. Still disoriented and unaware that Michael was also gone, she repeated the words. "They took her, Coop."

He took another step toward Beitermann and found his way blocked by Estevan. His words came through clenched teeth. "Why the hell didn't you stop them?"

Beitermann's head snapped up. "Because we didn't intend to die for any damned half-breed whore!" He went on, not caring what he said anymore, venting his feelings about Angela as well. "Because we didn't intend to die for any Indian's slut!"

Estevan spun around, facing the man. He felled him with a single blow. "This time, he was mine," he breathed, turning back to face Coop.

Regan was on her feet, her arms extended as she struggled to keep her balance. She shook her head, realizing finally the extent of the tragedy, her eyes searching the room for some sign of the older woman. Her gaze shifted to the place where she had last seen the younger Dundee woman.

And then she saw the dog. *Michael! They have taken Michael!*

She screamed a soul-wrenching cry that came from some secret place deep within her heart. "Michael! *MICHAEL!*"

Stunned by her sudden hysteria, Jonathan held her. He pulled her close, gently calling her name again and again as he tried to console her. Nothing worked. Feeling himself losing her to some terrible insanity, he shook her. "Stop it, Regan! Stop it!" There was a subtle change in her, an awareness in her eyes, and she began to come back to him. He felt her body restore itself as she slowly began to regain control, and he tried to encourage her with a small, unthinking remark. "He's your *nephew*, Regan—just your *nephew*." The words came out sounding harsher than he intended, and he hoped she understood.

But she pulled away from him, and the icy self-control returned. "He's my son," she announced, her voice firm. *"My son!"*

Estevan stood at the door, his rifle against his shoulder. Jonathan was already outside. "You'll wait for us, Coop?" Estevan asked. "Until we get back from Fort Lowell? Until we have some help from the military?"

Cooper didn't reply. He was working on the dog, an enamel pan of water at his knee. "You better get going, Estevan." He rinsed a piece of toweling and wrung it out. "You've got about four hours of daylight," he said, "and that's all."

Estevan lowered his head, considering the man's words. "Jonathan's going with me. We're going to take all four of the horses, Coop." There was a pause as he waited for some argument from the man. "We'll make better time. Short rides; change horses twice . . ."

"Just like we figured before," Cooper answered. He didn't even question the reason for Jonathan's going. The dog was on its feet now, and Cooper seemed to be concentrating all his effort and thought on examining the animal.

There was nothing more to say. Estevan backed out the door, reluctant to leave but knowing he had no choice. They were going to need help if they hoped to find Teresa and the others—a great deal of help.

He mounted one of the geldings, pulling himself up onto the animal's bare back and kicking it into a slow trot. Jonathan did likewise, and within minutes, the small, vulnerable convoy disappeared from view.

Chapter 11

It didn't take very long for the big dog to regain consciousness. After determining that the animal had suffered no lasting ill-effects other than a bump, Cooper and the dog started off to track down the raiders. Regan had been angry at Cooper for insisting she stay behind as she would only slow him down, and when he had left the hacienda, she had purposefully busied herself in the kitchen.

Cooper demonstrated no weariness, despite the fact that he had been walking for hours now. He was wearing mocassins and leather leggings; his boots were hanging from a strap around his neck. The huge black dog trotted along beside him, man and animal pacing themselves in anticipation of a long hunt. Together they moved across the edge of a saltlick, passing through the barren sands and entering the dense patch of cholla cactus beyond, following a wide trail.

Cooper felt his hair rise and brushed at the back of his neck, trying to sweep away a sensation that had been plaguing him for the last five miles. At first he thought it was the leather thong that held his boots in place, and he had eased up just long enough to place the thick strap behind his shirt collar. But the sensation was still there, more intense than before, and he could not brush it away.

He swung off the trail, picking his way into the thick scrub. The dog followed after him, a black shadow snaking through the brush as he patiently followed at Cooper's heel. The man's change in direction puzzled the animal, and he showed his unease with a series of high-pitched whines.

Cooper dropped to his knees and grabbed at the dog, pulling him close. Using his hand, he muzzled the animal. And then he waited.

The dog's head came up, his eyes bright as he picked up a new scent. The sound came then, the steady plod and scrape of a walking horse, and the dog's ears twitched. He tried to pull away from Cooper's hand, and the whining started anew. Cooper thumped the animal's nose with his knuckle. "Quiet!" he ordered, whispering the word, his tone harsh. Surprisingly, the dog obeyed.

The rider was moving slowly, his eyes riveted on the ground as he probed the hard shale for some sign. A second, riderless horse followed behind. Cooper watched as the man approached, angry as he recognized the animals as part of the horror he had left behind him: The stranger was riding one of the two Morgans that had bolted and was leading the other. *A straggler,* Cooper thought. *Someone left behind, no doubt, when he lost his own horse.*

Cooper waited until the man passed by him, keeping himself and the dog hidden among the thick mesquite. And then without warning, he made his move. He grabbed and yanked the man's leg.

He had estimated the man's weight from his height and was surprised to find that he had misjudged. The force of his sudden attack unseated the rider and tumbled them both into the dirt. The horses skittered off.

The men grappled, rolling down a small incline, and when they landed, Cooper spread-eagled the man beneath him. Then the man's hat fell away as he struggled against Cooper's strong hands, exposing a thick head of long black hair.

"You!" Cooper breathed. He realized his position then— the way he was straddling the woman—and leaped to his feet as if he had been sitting on fire.

She was wearing his old jeans again, and the same thin
chambray shirt. She righted herself, angry, brushing off the
dirt and debris from her hands and knees. "You've probably
cost us the horses," she complained. "And it took me over
an hour to recover them!"

"What the hell are you doing here?" he asked. He didn't
give a damn about the horses. At least, not right at the
moment.

She moved away from him and started climbing up the
incline. "They have my son," she retorted, not looking back.

Cooper scrambled after her. She moved amazingly well
and fast for a city-bred woman, and he was surprised. He was
unable to hide the surprise or the relief when he finally caught
up with her. The horses were there—both horses—and she
was already remounting. He gave her an unasked-for boost,
then without waiting to be asked, he mounted the other
animal.

"You presume a great deal, Mr. Dundee." She stared
straight ahead. "That horse is for Michael," she lied.

"Like hell," he groused. They moved out, staying abreast.
The dog trotted ahead of them, back on the hunt.

They didn't speak. Twice Cooper tried, but the words
failed to come. Instead he fumbled with the tack, making a
slow appraisal of the supplies the woman had packed. *And I
thought she was curled up in some corner bawling,* he
mused.

She had prepared well for the trip. Three canteens hung
from her own saddle, and three more from Cooper's. There
was a medical kit in a canvas sack, as well as a carefully
wrapped bottle that Cooper assumed to be liquor. Both rifle
scabbards carried repeating rifles, and he knew from the
weight that Regan's saddlebags contained extra rounds for
both weapons.

There was food, too—dried jerky and a supply of hardtack.
Cooper wondered how long it had taken her to pilfer all the
supplies. She would have had to go on pure woman's instinct,

guessing at the places where Teresa would keep her stores and supplies.

Regan rudely stopped Cooper's silent musings. She reached out, grabbing the cheek strap on his mount's bridle and pulling him up short. She didn't say anything, but just gave a subtle nod of her head to a place up the trail.

The dog was ahead of them. He stood stock still in the center of the trail, one paw lifted off the ground as if he had stopped midstep. Like a trained hunting dog, he struck a point, his nose lifted to the wind, the scent.

"We've got company," Cooper breathed. He dismounted, shaking his head at the woman as she began to do the same. One finger pressed against his lips, he warned her to be quiet. Giving her the reins to his mount, he unsheathed the Winchester and followed after the dog.

Together, Cooper and the animal padded down the narrow path at a ground-eating trot, keenly aware of every sound, every silence around them. There was the disturbed calling of the cactus wrens that darted and flew among the cholla, and then the rustle of wings as a covey of doves exploded from the brush far ahead.

Cooper broke off the trail, moving into the scrub. There were new sounds now, and he heard them even before the dog. Human voices. He followed the sound, dropping down in a low crouch as he neared the source.

There were three of them, all raiders. They were on foot, pausing beside the small trickle of a spring-fed creek that tumbled across the floor of the arroyo. Cooper watched as one of the men kneeled beside the stream.

The mercenary swore. He stared at his reflection in a pool of muddy water at the stream's edge and wiped at his face again. "This goddamn stuff is never going to come off," he growled. He gave up, swearing again, and stood up.

They seemed totally at ease. There was nothing to indicate that they thought they could have been followed—that they even worried about being followed. Thoroughly relaxed, they changed clothes, slipping into the more familiar denim pants and cotton work shirts. The headbands were discarded, as well as the moccasins and leather leggings, each man making the transformation from Indian to . . .

. . . *paid killer,* Cooper thought bitterly. Absently, he caressed the barrel of the Winchester and then changed his mind. Without knowing it, the three men would take him right where he wanted to go.

Impatiently, Regan waited for him. She stared ahead, listening for some sign, relieved when it finally came. The dog first, and then—right behind him—Cooper. His irregular gait alarmed her, but she said nothing.

"There are three of them," he said quietly. He started to mount his horse, grimacing as the pain tore through his upper leg to his groin, and made it on the second try.

"And now?" Regan asked.

"We're going to follow behind them," he answered. "We're going to let them lead us to what we're looking for."

"The Apaches," she said, thinking aloud.

He spun around in his saddle, angry. His eyes skimmed over her from head to toe, narrowing as they settled on her hands. Reaching out, he grabbed her wrist, no gentleness in him as he pressed against the tendons and forced her to display her fingers. "Look," he ordered, showing her the place with a quick flick of his eyes.

She did as she was told, seeing—for the first time—the accumulation of brown beneath her fingernails. Remembering how her fingernails had raked the face of the raider, she examined the residue more closely. Aloud she said, "Dye." There was the feel of oil and grit between her thumb and forefinger as she crumbled a piece of the dirt into a round chestnut smudge on her own skin.

He nodded his head, too proud to tell her that he was relieved by what he had discovered at the stream. Somehow he felt vindicated—that his suspicions of sabotage against the stage line were valid. And this vindicated his mother as well;

these were not her people who had attacked. Finally he said, "Paid mercenaries."

"But why?" She didn't—wouldn't—understand. "Why?"

"I'm not sure—yet," he replied.

They rode on without speaking, both of them grim faced and angry. The sinister game of hide and seek continued, Cooper again and again checking for signs: empty whiskey bottles here, a place beside the trail where the three men had stopped to relieve themselves; fresh horse droppings, still warm, lying in an even pattern that gave clear testimony to the horse's slow, plodding gait.

Occasionally Cooper had to dismount and lead his horse to follow the signs. He was limping again, the uneven gait more noticeable now than before, and Regan was concerned. Still, she said nothing, relieved when he was able to ride again but worried when she saw the effort it required for Cooper to climb aboard the horse.

It was getting dark, the gradual fading light drawing long shadows that made the landscape even more forbidding. The dog would be with them one moment, and then he would disappear, swallowed up in the black silhouettes cut by the dying sun. A thin crescent moon began its slow climb on the far horizon.

They were heading east now, not south as they had been, and the change in direction disturbed Cooper. He had assumed the raiders would head toward Tucson and the desert, taking the most direct route to the relative safety in the vast wasteland south of the Santa Cruz. The unexpected shift to the east affected Cooper's temperament, making him even more determined to push on.

It was her own fatigue as much as her growing worry about Cooper that prompted Regan's rebellion. She pulled her mount to a halt, winding the reins around the saddlehorn and using the bit when the animal's instinct to follow the other horse took hold. Chastising the animal, she forced him into a tight circle until she had regained control, and held him in place.

Cooper was a good hundred feet uptrail when he became conscious of the frantic whinings of the dog. The animal had dropped behind him and was racing between one horse and the other, confused, disconcerted. Swearing, Cooper pulled his own horse around and rode back.

He refused to spare her when he reined in next to her. "What's the matter, O'Rourke?" He hissed the words. "Too tired? Too hungry? Too damned weak?" His fingers grabbed hold of her arm, squeezing tightly.

Regan's response was calculated, intentional. Using her fist, she delivered a stout blow to the man's right thigh. Even in the fading light, in the shadowed space that separated them, Cooper's pain was evident. His face blanched, contorted, his eyes watering as he clenched his teeth against the surge of fire that raced through the long muscle in a dozen different directions. The hot skin began to cool under a renewed flood of warm blood.

She felt, rather than saw, the blood on her hand. Alarmed, she ordered him to dismount, angry when he answered her with a stoic shake of his head. "Fine, Mr. Dundee," she flared. "Bleed to death! And while you're doing it, you can think about your mercenaries and the games they're going to play with your mother and your sister!"

He considered her words. "Five minutes," he breathed, bargaining. "No longer."

"As long as it takes," she answered, refusing to be bound by his demands. She helped him dismount.

At her bidding, he dropped his pants, embarrassed that she found his hesitancy amusing. He sat down on the blanket she had spread on a flat boulder, surprised and relieved to find a gentleness in her that he never expected.

Using his pen knife, she probed carefully at the wound, extracting a flat, circular chunk of soft lead. She displayed it and then presented it to Cooper.

"Ricochet," he explained, panting slightly as the last wave of pain washed over him. He rolled the still-wet slug between his thumb and forefinger. "The bullet hits something solid, flattens out, and bounces off." He went silent again, watching as the woman doused his leg with a generous splash of disinfectant. He winced, shutting his eyes against the sting, and put the piece of lead into his vest pocket. "Who was Michael's father?" he asked. When she didn't answer, he asked the question a second time. "Michael's father. Who was he?"

She answered without thinking, her mind on the task at hand. "Someone very much like you." Immediately she recognized her error. She retaliated—both for her own foolishness in answering, and for his rudeness in asking—by pulling the bandage tight, giving the knot a final, vindictive tug.

She relented. "I was sixteen years old," she murmured, "in love with a fascinating older man. He had such endearing qualities." She was mocking herself, her own foolishness. "Loved dogs," she teased. "And children.

"His own children," she continued, the deprecating humor sharper than it was before. "He wouldn't marry me because he already had a wife," she finished. "So my brother and his wife took my baby, and I went east to go to school." She smoothed the bandage and stood up. "End of story," she breathed. There was nothing more to be said.

They resumed their journey over Regan's loud objections. This time, Cooper responded more civilly. "They'll make camp for the night," he said. "They don't know they're being followed, so they'll take it easy." He smiled, and the bloodlust came back into his eyes. "And they won't be expecting any company," he finished.

It was almost dawn when they discovered Delgado's campsite. Still limping badly, Cooper made a quick reconnaissance of the area.

Delgado had been careless. He had chosen his campsite for comfort and convenience, bedding down on the sandy embankment of a summer-dry riverbed. Stripped of their saddles and blankets, the horses were picketed far away from the men. From Cooper's vantage place in the rocks above the arroyo, the campsite had the look of a recreational expedition—a rich man's foray into the wilderness to hunt wild animals.

Cooper returned to the place where Regan and the dog were waiting. He came into their hiding place at a hobbling run, alarmed to see the woman struggling to subdue the dog.

She gasped, winded from her battle to hold the dog in place, "I think he senses that we're close to Michael."

Cooper took the dog in hand. Using his belt, he fashioned a makeshift collar and leash. He knew from the way the dog was behaving that they would need a muzzle to keep him from giving them away. Regan anticipated his needs. She turned away from him, quickly unbuttoning her shirt. Unable to turn away—not really wanting to turn away—Cooper watched as she removed the shirt, then the camisole beneath the shirt. Her naked back, the whiteness of her skin, and the sensual movement of her arms, captivated him.

She put the shirt back on, clutching the front closed as she turned around, and handed him the lacy undergarment. It was like gossamer against his fingertips, and he held it for a time, fingering the satin ribbon that was laced through the eyelet that made up the shoulder straps. His smile broadened when he saw the look of chagrin that colored her cheeks and painted them bright red. She lowered her eyes and fumbled with the buttons as she fastened the shirtfront.

He made a noose by tearing the cotton camisole into strips and knotting them together. The dog struggled, and he was forced to straddle the animal in order to put the muzzle in place. He used a slipknot to fasten it, knowing that when the time came he would need the dog's teeth. Finished, he stepped back and proudly displayed his handiwork.

Then, quietly, Coop outlined his plan. Surprise was the single advantage they would have in the face of such overwhelming odds. He had counted fifteen men in the camp now, including the three stragglers who had ridden in just prior to his quick explorations. "We can have no mistakes, Regan. No time for second thoughts." He then handed her the Henry repeating rifle. "Do you know how to use this?" he asked.

She inhaled, biting on her bottom lip, her eyes on the ground. Her answer also explained her expertise when she had ridden the gelding during their games: "I grew up in Kansas, Coop. During the War. There were six of us still at home when my father—" her expression changed, became hard "—when my father disappeared. If we wanted meat on the table, we had to find it. Or steal it. No matter how we got it, we then had to kill it." Poverty and shame had given her the drive to climb up and out of the dirt.

"You're going to be killing *men* this time, Regan." Cooper let the words sink in. He was remembering a time back at the house when Regan and Angela shared a place at a gunport; they had been reluctant to fire.

"I told you before, Coop. They have my son," she whispered. "I intend to get him back."

Absently, he offered her a shot of brandy, surprised when she took a long drink before handing the bottle back. He emptied it, then gently laid it down in the dirt. For a moment he stood in place, rocking back and forth on his game leg as he waited for the brandy to kill the pain. "All right," he breathed. "Let's go."

They easily made their way by moonlight to the rocks above the campsite, then leashed the dog to a bush. Dropping down on their bellies, they began their assault, deadly accurate as they opened fire on the prone figures of the sleeping men.

On the far side of the camp, Delgado sprang to his feet, roused from a sound slumber, and just as quickly scrambled back across the clearing. Taking cover behind the pile of saddles at the picket lines, he began firing. Behind him, away from the warmth of the fires, Teresa, Angela, and Michael huddled among the rocks.

Teresa tore at the rawhide thongs that bound her wrists, using her teeth. The wet leather was salty against her tongue, and she worked quickly. One by one, she pulled the knots loose, until—at last—her hands were free.

She ignored the cords still binding her slim ankles and crawled to her daughter. Nimbly, her fingers picked at the bindings, and she freed the young woman's hands. "Your feet, Angela." Her voice was filled with a degree of panic that she was unable to conceal. "You must untie your feet!" Already, she had turned her attentions to Michael. The boy was on his knees, holding out his hands. She loosened the straps that bound his wrists, grateful that the kidnappers had seen no need to bind the boy's feet. "Run, Michael! *Run!*"

But Delgado was on his own feet. He spied the boy and sprinted after him.

At that moment, Cooper released the dog. A single jerk tore away the makeshift muzzle, then the belt came free as the animal bolted from beneath Cooper's fingers. The animal tore down the face of the small cliff, oblivious to everything but the figure of the running boy, his body low to the ground as he raced into the clearing. Cooper and Regan followed in the dog's wake.

In the distance, Delgado saw the dog, saw the feral fury of the animal's head-on charge. "Dundee." He cursed aloud, recognizing Cooper following after the dog. Turning away from the boy, he stopped his pursuit and reversed direction, disappearing behind the picket lines.

Breed Tatum was hurriedly saddling the horses, Benito Chavez working with him. "Where are the women?" Delgado roared. He pointed to the place where Angela and Teresa had been tethered, furious that they were gone. Then, in the rocks at the opening of the small canyon, he saw a flash of color and watched as Teresa stumbled and fell. "There!" he shouted. "Over there!"

He mounted the long-legged pinto at a run, swinging up

into the saddle. Kicking the horse into a full run, he pursued the two women as Tatum and Chavez followed behind.

The terrain was rough and rocky, the floor of the canyon littered with the debris and litter of the spring floods. Ankle-deep sand impeded the women's progress, their long skirts snagging and catching on dead tree limbs. For every yard they gained, they lost another; their labored breathing was as loud as the pounding of their hearts.

A great piercing pain swelled in Teresa's chest, and she stumbled. Angela turned back to her, collapsing into the sand beside her mother as she tried to help her stand. "Please, Mother," she sobbed. "Please!"

Teresa waved the girl away. "Run, Angela. You must run!"

"No!" The girl's refusal was quick, resolute. "Get up, Mama," she begged. "We've got to hide, Mama, until Coop can find us!"

Teresa struggled to her feet. The pain was still there, and spreading, reaching a point in her back just below the shoulder blades. She closed her eyes against the soreness and grabbed her daughter's hand. "All right, darling," she breathed. "All right." Together they moved on, both of them weaker now, their wind gone.

Delgado came upon them at a full run. He relished the pursuit, watching as they tried vainly to scramble away from him. Tatum and Chavez joined the game, herding the women as if they were cattle, working them closer and closer to the steep sides of the canyon.

Delgado reached down, grabbing a handful of Angela's long hair. He tore her away from Teresa's outstretched arms, lifting her up off the ground.

Both women attacked him, Angela first, her nails tearing at the flesh on his arms and neck. Teresa's assault was even more vicious. She lunged at the man, her teeth sinking into the tender flesh at the back of his leg. She drew blood, rejoicing in the pain she caused him, and bit at him again.

"Take her!" He still held Angela's hair. Viciously, he pulled the young woman away from his face, holding her well off the ground. Tatum grabbed her around the waist and pulled her away.

The pain in Delgado's leg increased as Teresa attacked again, more savage than before. He drew his pistol, leveling the weapon at the woman's head, and fired.

The hammer fell on an empty chamber. For a long moment, Teresa and Delgado faced each other, both of them surprised that she still lived. The woman recovered more quickly than the man, a desperation in her as she realized his intentions. She reached out, grabbing a handful of flesh beneath the pinto's belly, her strong hands twisting the vulnerable tenderness at the horse's genitals.

The animal screamed and reared straight up in the air, his front feet flailing as he struck out at an unseen attacker. Teresa grabbed at him again, applying even more pressure, and the animal tumbled over on his back.

Delgado slid out of the saddle. He landed on his back and rolled away, springing to his feet. Already Tatum and Chavez were disappearing into the brush ahead of them. He saw Teresa then, the smug smile that she wore. He grappled for his holster, remembering that the gun was empty, and then reached for the knife. There was no sound from the clearing now, and he knew the others were dead. He would need time to get away from Dundee.

He overtook Teresa, catching her long skirts and dragging her down into the dirt beneath him. Coldly, he straddled her, moving well down on her legs as he held her in place, one hand closing around her throat.

He stabbed her, driving the blade of his knife through the thickness of her dress, opening a long shallow wound meant to expose her intestines. There was a slow deliberation in his move, his hand stifling her screams. He watched her face, saw the pain and terror in her eyes, and felt the satisfaction of knowing that she was totally aware of what he had done to her: *She would take a long time dying.*

Smiling, he stood up, wiping the blade of his knife on the hem of her skirt. "Senora," he grinned, mocking her as he bowed. And then he mounted the horse and was gone.

The woman lay there, the tears streaming down her face as she cried—not for herself, but for her daughter. And for Cooper. Especially for Cooper. He would find her, and he would stay with her, and he would watch her die. If she could only hide; if she could only find the strength to crawl away. . . .

Chapter 12

Around them, arms outstretched, lay the dead. The smell and taste of death was heavy on the air as Regan moved among the fallen, numb and silent as she viewed the carnage. Michael and the dog stayed close at her side.

"I'll need your spare cartridges." Cooper avoided looking at the woman. "You've got the boy," he said. "You can go back to the ranch."

She shook her head. "They still have your mother, Coop. And Angela." She was silent a moment, her fingers toying with Michael's hair. "I'm going with you," she said finally. When he tried to protest, she reasoned, "I can help you."

"What about Michael?" he argued. His eyes swept the boy. Michael had already seen more death than most men see in their entire lifetimes.

Regan stared out at the campsite. Already, the green bottleflies had begun to swarm. "He survived this," she said. "He'll survive whatever else may come."

She left him then, moving across the clearing, carefully picking her way among the dead as she set about salvaging the things they could use. More firearms. Blankets. The horses. Carefully, she approached the string of unsaddled horses that still remained tethered at the long picket line. Cooper joined her, and together they worked through the mounts, picking the ones most suitable for their needs. When they were done, they had chosen five from the dozen that remained: two fresh mounts for themselves, a horse for Michael, and the animals they would need to carry Angela and Teresa.

If we find them. The unspoken thought passed between the man and the woman, and they shared a long glance. Regan finally excused herself. The stench of blood filled her nose, and she needed to get away. Cooper understood. He touched her arm. "I'll saddle up," he said. "Michael can help me."

She nodded, grateful that he had not made fun of her weakness. Eyes straight ahead, she moved off into the canyon; she knew that this was the direction they would take and that Cooper would catch up to her with the horses. She walked slowly, sloughing through the sand, following the clear trail left by Delgado and the others. Rounding a small bend, she paused, leaning against a rock to take a much-needed drink of water. Though she forced herself to look back in the direction she had come, she was relieved that the brush and scrub prevented her from seeing.

Something roused her, an unnatural sound competing with the birds and the constant buzzing hum of the insects. There was a subtle fluttering of fabric being lifted by the wind. . . .

She found Teresa. There was a long trail of wet sand where she had dragged herself away from the riverbed, her supreme effort marked by the tracks of her hands and feet. She had crawled into the brush, inch by agonizing inch.

"Teresa." Regan called her name, softly. "Oh, Teresa!"

The older woman turned over on her back, her hand clutching at her lower abdomen. A smear of dried blood covered the front of her dress, her fingers.

Regan dropped to her knees. Gently, she placed her hand on the woman's forehead. Teresa's eyelids fluttered and opened, her eyes focusing as she tried to smile. "You mustn't tell Coop," she whispered. "Promise me, you won't tell Coop."

But Regan shook her head, her own eyelids fluttering as she forced back tears. She could hear the sound of the horses, the steady, slow rise and fall of the shod hooves coming in even cadence. She stood up, exposing herself. "Coop!" she yelled.

He dismounted, tersely ordering Michael to stay put. He knew deep in his gut even before he saw. "Mother?"

They had been at the army post near Tucson just the few minutes it took to tell their story, and Estevan already realized—as the officer listened to Jonathan's words—that it made no difference that he and Jonathan had their doubts that the attackers had been Indians, the officer's mind had already been made up.

"We'll assemble a full company," he said, snapping the same order at an aide. Benevolently, he placed his arm around Jonathan's shoulder. "Obviously, we are dealing with reservation bucks on a raiding spree," he said, as pompous as he was pigheaded. "We'll make short work of them, sir," he promised. "By God, we'll make short work of them!"

Estevan shook his head. The aide disappeared into an anteroom, and before the man could close the door, Estevan caught sight of a civilian clerk who was already pumping the soldier for information. The young legislator made no effort to conceal his contempt. He knew—before the troop was mounted and ready—the word would already be spread, the report exaggerated. Before it was over, the whole territory would burn with Apache fever. He pushed himself away from the wall. "I'm going with you, Major," he announced. He refused to be put off. Expectantly he turned to Jonathan.

The elder Dundee shook his head. "I'm going on to Tucson," he said finally. "To the office." Something he had seen had confirmed his worst suspicions, and he couldn't make the image go away: the big pinto he had seen riding away from the *rancheria*, the flash of black and white that disappeared among the other animals.

He knew that he had seen Ramón Delgado's horse.

*   *   *

Cooper was beside his mother, hunkered down in the dirt by her shoulder. She raised her hand, touching his arm, fighting the pain as she talked. "You've got to go, Coop," she begged. "You've got to find Angela. . . ."

Subbornly, he shook his head. He knew that her wound was fatal and that there was nothing he could do—but he would not leave. Not now. Not yet. "No," he whispered.

She was crying. The wound in her belly didn't hurt anymore; instead there was an inner pain, a sorrow deep in her chest that caused her the greatest hurt. Visions of Angela—of the things that could be happening to Angela—tore at her heart. "Please, Coop," she implored. "You can't help me anyway, Cooper," she chided. "I'm going to die, and nothing you can do will change that." She turned her head, searching for Regan and finding her among the rocks. Michael was in her lap, asleep. "Leave Regan here," Teresa whispered. "She can stay with me until . . ." The woman wet her lips. "Until you find Angela," she finished.

Again Cooper refused. "I won't leave you." There was a gentle determination in his voice that Teresa recognized as being so like Malachai. With that, he stood up, going a few feet off to gather some dead branches. Quickly he built the frame for a small lean-to, using a blanket to create a shelter for Teresa from the hot sun.

She sighed, resigned that he would stay with her to the end, and hating herself for taking so long to end it. She accepted his decision and was silent.

The silence was worse than the labored conversation. Cooper struggled against the fatigue that was turning his body to lead, his eyelids drooping. Twice he dozed off, jolting awake as his mind refused to sleep. A fly buzzed around his head, and another crawled across his hand, drawn by the smell of blood and bile. Angrily, he tried to shoo them away, watching as they flew off in search of the source of the odor that had attracted them. They landed on Teresa's skirt and disappeared into the folds of her dress.

The incessant hum of the insects worked its hypnotic magic. Regan and Michael were already asleep, and Cooper was also surrendering to the spell. His lids grew heavy again, and his head dropped to his chest. He tried to stay awake and failed, the physical and spiritual exertion of the past hours destroying his will.

Teresa watched as her son slept, measuring the deep rise and fall of his chest and the quiet sound of his breathing. She waited, grateful for the small shelter he had constructed, her eyes lovingly caressing his face. She saw the hurt there and hated it, knowing that her suffering was the cause for his pain.

With her free hand, she reached out, silently easing her son's revolver from its holster. She said her silent good-byes to her son and her God, burying the pistol in the folds of her skirt to muffle the sound as she cocked it, and lifted the gun to her chin. Nestling the barrel in the hollow between her jaw and her throat, she pulled the trigger.

Delgado felt the uneven up and down movement of the pinto's shoulders as the animal began favoring its right leg. He reined in and dismounted, examining the horse's right hoof. A stone lay wedged against the sole, the sharp fragment partially imbedded in the inflamed tissue. The mercenary cursed and let the foot drop, ground-hitched the horse, and waited. He used the time to reload his pistol.

Breed Tatum soon rounded the small bend and urged his horse up the incline, pulling up when he came even with Delgado. "Trouble, *jefe*?" He shifted to a more comfortable position, his arm tight around Angela's small waist.

Delgado shook his head. He took a long drink from his canteen and offered it to his subordinate. "Where's Chavez?" he asked.

Tatum finished his drink before he answered. He jerked his head in the direction from which he had just come. "His horse pulled up lame," he said. "Just after we came through

the water." He wiped his mouth and handed the canteen back
to Delgado. "He's on foot. If he's smart, he'll head into the
high country."

Delgado nodded. He squatted down, opening a packet of
jerked beef he had taken out of his saddlebags. He looked up
and saw the concern on Tatum's face and grinned. "We've
got time," he said. His eyes shifted to the girl. "The old
woman's dead," he announced, taking a bite of the beef.
"Well, almost dead."

Tatum grinned. He grabbed the girl's breasts and gave
them a squeeze. His finger traced the crude gag at her mouth,
and he used his thumb to wipe away the stream of tears that
rolled down her cheeks. He slipped off the horse and helped
himself to the supply of meat. "How much time?" he asked.
He was thinking of the girl.

There was a sound next to his ear, the cold click of metal
working against metal. Delgado pressed the pistol against
Tatum's temple. "How much time you have is up to you,
niño." He backed away, pulling the rifle from its sheath on
his saddle. "I need the horse," he said. "And I need the
girl."

Tatum was careful to keep his hands right where they
were. "Leave me a gun," he said. "Somewhere up the way,
leave me a gun."

Delgado nodded, pulling Tatum's pistol from its holster.
"Okay," he said, "I'll leave the pistol and rifle up ahead."
He felt magnanimous. "And a canteen." The smile came and
went. "Don't move, compadre. You stay right where you
are until we're gone."

Tatum nodded. "I know this country, jefe. I'll find my
way out of here." He was reassuring Delgado, bargaining
with him. "Better alive and on foot than dead," he finished.

The mercenary leader mounted the dark gelding. He checked
the two canteens that hung from the saddlehorn and, satisfied
that they were almost full, took his leave. He made the ride
out of the scrub slowly, one arm around the girl and on the

reins, the other holding the rifle. He kept looking back at Tatum until the man was out of sight. Despite his promises, he left nothing behind.

Cooper was awake instantly, the acrid scent of gunpowder pungent in the air around him as the sound of the single shot reverberated against the walls of the arroyo. It echoed and reechoed down the canyon, fading into the horizon, lingering like the roll of distant thunder.

He crawled beside the still form of his mother. She was dead, her eyes partially rolled back in a glassy stare, the light gone. His hands trembled, and he reached out to her, his fingers raised above her shattered head. "Sweet Jesus," he begged, feeling her sticky blood turning cold against his skin. His head exploded, the thumping of his pulse growing loud in his ears until he could no longer control the screams that burst from his mouth. He sat there, shouting curses into the emptiness that surrounded him until he was exhausted. And then he buried his head against her breast, his shoulders stiffening in protest to the sobs that shook his body.

From her place in the shelter of the rocks, Regan watched, holding Michael's head in her lap. Cooper's bent form—the posture of defeat that seemed to shrink his entire body—made him appear more vulnerable than she ever thought possible. His terrible, heart-wrenching pain was etched in his every feature. She knew from the sporadic rise and fall of his broad shoulders that he was weeping, and she longed to reach out and comfort him. Yet she could not. His was a solitary pain. He was alone with his mother—alone in his grief—and she could not intrude.

Finally, Cooper rose from the place beside his mother. His movements were steady, a mechanical sureness in each measured step as he tended to his mother's needs.

Regan watched as he fashioned a shroud from the blankets in his bedroll. His face was remote, drawn; but his hands and fingers were steady. He finished his chore and then hoisted the body onto the dun mare. His hand lingered for a long time on Teresa's blanketed shoulder. Leaving Michael with the dog, she joined him.

"Coop . . ." she began. She bit her lip, stopping the tears that burned at her eyes and throat, and knew that there was nothing—nothing at all—she could say to him.

"I want you to take her home, Regan," he said finally. The words were as distant, as emotionless, as his expression.

Her first instinct was to argue—as they always argued—her mouth opening, then closing, as she reconsidered. "Come back with me," she pleaded, already knowing he would not.

He shook his head. "She wants me to find Angela," he breathed, as if the woman were still alive. He tried to avoid looking at the covered form that rested on the horse's back, but could not. "Now, Regan. I've got to find her now."

The intensity of his words—the sudden change in his eyes—frightened her. There was a hungry, predatory look on his face and a terrible contained rage that was smoldering just beneath the surface. "Please wait, Coop," Regan implored. "Jonathan and Estevan will soon be bringing help."

It was as if he had not heard her words—as if he had chosen not to hear her words. "I want you to take the other horses," he said. When he saw that she didn't understand, he explained—slowly, as if he were talking to a child. "I'll need them later, Regan. To pull the coach."

He didn't wait for her reply. Instead, he quickly began stripping the saddle from one of the animals they had taken from the renegades' campsite. He intended to travel light and fast. Grimacing at the pain in his right leg, he vaulted onto the gelding's broad back.

Before he was able to leave, Regan touched his leg gently. The realization that she might never see him again tore at her soul. "Be careful, Coop." She inhaled, trying desperately to erase the fear. "Please be careful. . . ." The words faded into nothingness, and she felt the man slip beneath her fingers. She watched after him as he disappeared into the dense undergrowth, and she felt terribly alone.

For the boy's sake, she composed herself, forcing a calmness she didn't feel. She called out to Michael and pulled him close in a tight hug when he came running over. "We're going to take Coop's mother home, Michael," she said softly. "You and I are going to take Teresa home. . . ."

Cooper touched his heels to the gelding's flanks, his body becoming one with the horse's as the animal dropped into a full run. The trail he followed led toward the distant horizon, the tracks left by Delgado and the others spreading before him as plainly as a surveyor's red line on a parchment map.

Their flight followed the natural course of the dry riverbed, the wall of the canyon rising high above the yellow sand. For a distance of more than ten miles, there was nothing but the freshly rutted earth and the steep, barren cliffs. Gradually the terrain changed as the lofty walls began to diminish, the riverbed widening into a broad expanse of desert flatland. A bubbling, spring-fed pool appeared, a narrow ribbon of shallow, clear water cutting through the sand to expose a rough bed of shale and limestone.

The tracks of the three horses converged and disappeared into the water. Cooper's pace slackened, and he pulled the horse to an abrupt halt. He let it drink, quenching his own thirst with the tepid, metallic-tasting water from his canteen. His eyes narrowed as he scanned the landscape looking for signs, but there was nothing, the desert floor unblemished for as far as he could see in any direction.

He remained mounted and urged his horse into a slow walk, cursing his inability to find any tracks. The sound of his own voice startled him. Suddenly he was conscious of his aloneness, an increased awareness opening his mind to the actuality of his mother's death. The blessed numbness that had taken hold of him when he first realized she was dead was now gone. He could see her again—see her belly ripped open, the agony drawing terrible lines in her face.

She had been gutted, purposely maimed and torn by someone who meant for her to die a slow death. Someone who had left her knowing that she would remain aware—horribly aware—until the very end. He knew that the raiders were not Apache—that at least most of them were not Apache. And yet his mother had been brutalized in a way familiar to her own people. *To his own people.*

Cooper thought of the faceless dead that lay behind him— the men that he and Regan had slaughtered as they slept. They meant nothing to him; their deaths meant nothing to him. He wanted to see the face of the man who had murdered his mother. He wanted to watch that face as the man died. . . . Resolute, he resumed his search.

Delgado was on foot, leading his horse as he picked his way down the side of a rock-strewn hill. He paused at the bottom of the incline, greedily sucking the last of his water from the dented canteen, and turned back to the woman still mounted on the horse. Gingerly, he reached out, his hand crawling up her ankle and disappearing beneath her skirt. He wanted her to know what was in store for her once they were away from this place and he had time to instruct her in the ways of a proper whore. She would, he knew, fetch a good price in the border houses that catered to men who found their secret delights in the services and attentions of a fair-skinned, fair-haired *gringa*.

Angela did not pull away from the man's probing fingers. She had made that mistake once—only once. He had dragged her from the horse and had brutalized her, doing with his teeth and mouth what Tatum and the others had tried to do with their hands. The pain and the humiliation of his assault was still as intense now as it had initially been. Raw, red lines furrowed the tender skin at her neck and on the naked skin of her right shoulder and breast. She bit down hard on the knotted cloth that still bound her mouth, closing her eyes and her mind to the man's obscene investigations.

Their silent sojourn began again, Delgado still on foot. An insidious, eerie panic had seized him—the peculiar fear of a man who found himself in a place that was strange, yet somehow familiar. He wiped a sweaty palm across his dry mouth, staring out at the landscape.

The hoofprints of his own horse mocked him. They spread out before him, leading off into the place from which he had just come, a stark reminder of his folly.

He had made a complete circle. Without knowing it—with the sun standing high noon above him—he had retraced his own steps through the hard-packed clay and had returned to the banks of the small stream.

The sound came to him then, the steady drumming of a shod horse bearing down on him at full run. Another noise reached out to him, the primal cry of a savage hunter who had found his prey and longed to drink its blood.

Cooper saw and could not believe. It was as if the gods had answered all his prayers and, in apology for their recent unjust punishments, had made him a gift of his quarry. He bore down on the man, unmindful of Delgado's drawn weapon.

In desperation, Delgado tried to blunt the fury of Cooper's head-on assault. He bolted, disappearing behind his horse and using the girl as a shield. He fought to hold onto the animal and cursed Angela as she purposely dug her heels into the gelding's sides. Swearing, he struck out at the young woman's exposed calf with the barrel of his pistol.

It was as if Cooper didn't see his sister, as if he was no longer aware that she was there. He cruelly whipped his horse as he urged it on at a full gallop.

A collision seemed inevitable. And then, of its own accord,

Cooper's horse suddenly turned; its rider did not. Cooper used the momentum of the running horse, catapulting from its back in a headfirst lunge that carried him across the back end of Delgado's terrified mount. His shoulder grazed Angela, and she was knocked from the saddle. She crashed to the ground, momentarily stunned, oblivious to the pandemonium only inches from her head.

The force of Cooper's airborn assault was tempered by his collision with the woman, but Delgado was still lifted up and off his feet when Cooper smashed into his chest. Together, the two men flew through the air, a shower of sand and gravel exploding above and around them as they tumbled to the ground.

There was a deafening roar as Delgado's cocked pistol discharged, both men feeling the heat of burning powder as the bullet whistled past their ears. Cooper's fingers dug into the long tendon at Delgado's wrist, and he forced the man's hand open. The pistol dropped into the dirt and was buried beneath both men as they rolled and grappled their way across the rough ground.

They exchanged a flurry of blows, too close to do each other any real harm. And then a subtle change occurred. Cooper's whole body seemed transformed, the desperation and futile rage of only moments before replaced by a cold, methodical sense of purpose and determination. He was beneath Delgado, flat on his back in the hot sand. Using both hands, he clutched the outlaw's strong upper arms, one hand at each shoulder. Slowly—forcefully—he lifted Delgado away from his chest.

Cooper was smiling. His fingers were knotted in the tender flesh above Delgado's collarbones, his thumbs digging into the distended veins at the man's throat. The effect was paralyzing. Delgado's arms and hands went numb as an electrifying tingle coursed through his flesh to the very tips of his fingers. And then the pain came, and the intense agony

evoked a loud moan that came from between clenched teeth.
The muted whine rose to a terrible shriek of new pain as
Cooper jerked his knee upward into the man's crotch.

Cooper threw the man aside and sprang to his feet. He
kicked out at Delgado's bent head, missing as the Mexican
rolled away from him. The mercenary's hands shot out and
his fingers closed around Cooper's ankle; although still weak,
he tenaciously held on, giving Cooper's booted foot a sudden
twist.

Both men were on their knees now, facing each other.
Cooper swung from the ground, his fist cutting through the
air to connect with Delgado's chin. The man's head snapped
back, blood pouring from his mouth as his teeth closed on his
tongue. Instinctively, he wiped the back of his hand across
his lips, a bright smear of red coloring his dark flesh. But his
hand came away from the wound in a powerful backhand
sweep, and his wet knuckles collided with Cooper's jaw,
leaving a smear of deep crimson. In one smooth move, the
hand disappeared behind his back.

The sun caught the sudden flash of steel as Delgado drew
a knife. His movements were fluid and sure, a macabre
beauty in the sudden grace of his long fingers as he made
his attack.

Cooper sucked in his lean belly and heard the whispering
sound of the blade ripping into his shirt just above his belt.
There was a thin trickle of blood and the stinging pain of
salty sweat on raw tissue. The realization of what had almost
happened renewed Cooper's resolve. He saw the wound and
thought of Teresa—and the terrible rage returned.

He grabbed Delgado's wrist with both hands, ignoring the
long blade. Rising up from the sand, he held on, forcing the
renegade's body back, the sound of their labored breathing
punctuating the still air. Cooper kept applying pressure, using
the weight of his entire body as he slowly rose to his feet.
Delgado's back arched, and he felt himself being driven into

the ground. The elbow of his right hand locked as Cooper continued to force his arm up and back, and he reached out with his left hand in a desperate effort to keep his balance. There was a terrible pain in the small of his back, and he heard the dry noise of his spine cracking in rebellion to the continued stretch and strain of his forced backward descent.

Delgado fell over, sideways, his legs unfolding from beneath his buttocks as he collapsed on his back into the dirt. Cooper stood over him, his legs spread, his hands still locked around Delgado's extended arm. He kept twisting, bending the wrist back, the sudden snap of bone rousing him from the trancelike reverie. He caught the knife as it tumbled from Delgado's limp fingers, his left hand closing around the rawhide-bound haft.

Cooper dropped to his knees, straddling Delgado's prone form, totally disregarding the man's cries of pain. Fascinated, he juggled the knife in his palm as if testing it for balance, the sun glinting off the clean blade. For the first time, the flash of cognizance touched his eyes, and he recognized Ramón Delgado, right-hand man to Logan Montgomery—Jonathan's Logan Montgomery. "You," he breathed, turning his gaze on Delgado. *"You!"* Reaching out, he lifted the man's shirt, exposing the light brown flesh of his taut stomach.

He plunged the knife into Delgado's belly, just below and to the right of his navel. Coldly, watching the man's eyes, he made a quick incision.

Delgado's stomach convulsed, the wound opening and exposing his torn intestines. His single, long scream shattered the unnatural silence, his head rocking back and forth as he tried to deny the reality of the thing that Cooper had done.

Cooper stood up. He watched indifferently as Delgado's finger clawed at the dirt in search of his half-buried pistol. Fighting the pain, the outlaw raised up on one elbow, extending his arm until the weapon was just within his reach.

Cooper, however, plucked it from beneath Delgado's fingers.

He stood above the man, slowly rotating the cylinder as he ejected the live cartridges one at a time, until only one remained in the chamber. "A gift," he said softly, tossing the weapon into the dirt away from Delgado's reach. "From my mother," he finished. He turned his back on the man and walked away.

A strange metamorphosis took place as Cooper approached Angela. His stride—his very countenance—began to change and soften. Even his voice was different—a tender, soothing resonance replacing the flat, cold monotone. He reached down and removed the gag from his sister's mouth, his hand lingering on her cheek. "It's all right, Angela," he murmured. "You're going to be all right." He used Delgado's knife to cut the thongs that bound her wrists, then shoved the knife into his belt.

"Mother's dead, isn't she?" Angela's voice was flat, dull. She already knew the answer to her question. The tears began—silent, angry tears that would not purge her inner pain. "Kill him," she breathed. She wrapped her arms around herself and drew her knees up against her belly, her entire body shaking as she was taken with a sudden, unnatural chill. Cooper reached out to comfort her, but she flinched, pulling away from his touch. "Kill him!" she ordered, her voice rising hysterically. *"Kill him now!"*

Cooper scooped Angela up in his arms, holding her close to his chest. She beat at him with her fists, angry that Delgado still lived, but finally she knew the welcome release of real tears.

Delgado was weeping, too. He called out to the pair, watching as they mounted the horses. His voice rose as he shouted Cooper's name, cursing him; the anger then gave way to a long, anguished sob as the pain in his belly worsened and robbed him of his voice. "In the name of God, Dundee," he croaked, pleading with the man. *"In the name of God! . . ."* He heard the sound of the horses' hooves as Cooper and

Angela kicked the animals into a full run, and heard that sound diminish into nothingness.

The silence mocked him—just as the loaded pistol that lay a full ten feet away from his outstretched fingers mocked him. Desperately, he rolled onto his side and began an agonizing crawl toward the weapon, the sand beneath him growing wet with blood and water. He began to pray for a speedy death.

Chapter 13

Twilight had already begun to paint its long shadows across the desert floor. Regan stood at the front door of the Dundee hacienda, her gaze fastened on the dark horizon east of the house. Behind her, she could hear Aaron Beitermann and the other legislators as they quarreled, and knew that she was the source of their current displeasure. She spoke to them without turning around. "You aren't going to take the horses, Mr. Beitermann." Her voice was firm, unwavering, as full of tenacity as her words.

Beitermann swore, and his curses were echoed by the three men at his back. "You listen here, missy," he began, shaking his finger at the woman. "I've . . ." He reconsidered and began again. "*We've* got business in Tucson." He threw up his hands in disgust. "Our homes are in Tucson," he argued.

Regan turned her head, staring at the man. Her gaze then slowly shifted to the others. "Cooper will take you to Tucson," she announced. "Dundee Transport will take you to Tucson." She ignored Beitermann's loud guffaw and turned away, knowing that—for all intents and purposes—there was no Dundee Transport. Not anymore.

Michael was her greatest concern now. She stared out into the growing darkness of the front porch, thinking how small and vulnerable the boy looked. He was sitting on an upturned keg, the dog's head resting on his knee. His face was pointed toward the hidden places where he had known so much terror, and he was sucking his thumb.

It had taken Regan considerable time before she finally realized that in all the time that had passed since she and Cooper found him—even during their long ride home—he had not spoken one word. The long silence worried her, just as the boy's strange detachment and lack of emotion worried her.

She hated this feeling of absolute helplessness. Nothing she did for her son seemed to help, and she was unable to penetrate the invisible wall that surrounded him.

Her feelings of impotence increased even more when she thought of Cooper. The quiet torment of waiting was worse than the hell she had experienced in the canyon. At least then she had been able to help him, had known what to do, what to expect. But now. . .

The dog was first to hear the sound. His ears lifted, although his head was still immobile on the boy's lap, then his nose twitched as he picked up a familiar scent. Twice, his great tail rose and fell, thumping softly as he waited for some sign from the boy that he could go. At first Michael remained unaware of the dog's subtle moves. Then he stopped sucking his thumb, and his head cocked as he stared into the distant haze. He slipped off the keg, slowly moving toward the sound.

Hearing the faraway sound, Regan came out of the house, her eyes on the boy and the dog. She paused in the doorway, uncomfortable memories assaulting her, and she instinctively reached for the rifle. "Michael!" she called, alarmed that the boy was now so far from the house.

The big dog raced into the sparse scrub just beyond the clearing, the boy following after him at a slow trot. Then the child's pace increased, and his arms pumped at his sides as he followed the dog at a run. Regan felt a sudden panic. There was a long, terrifying moment when the boy disappeared behind the increasingly thick vegetation, and she sprinted after him.

She could hear him ahead of her, his feet pounding against the packed clay as he tore through the dry brush. There was the brittle, dry snap of small branches being torn away from stout limbs, and then another, different sound. Regan felt the ground beneath her tremble slightly, the sound of the hooves close now.

Michael's voice reached out to her, his voice rose sweet and clear on the air. "Coop!" There was a slight pause, and then the noise of his excited breathing. "Coop!"

Cooper dismounted at a run. His freed mount tore past Michael, the dog nipping at its heels as he drove it toward the house. Cooper followed in the animal's wake, his arms opening wide as he swept the boy off his feet. He carried the child with him, his pace never slackening, his free arm closing tightly around Regan's waist as she ran to meet him.

His kiss was long—harsh, yet caring. It was as if there was a great hunger within the man that only Regan could satisfy, and he held her for a long time. When he finally released her, he backed away. He saw the rifle and raised his hands in mock horror. "Sorry," he apologized. It was a poor lie.

Regan inhaled sharply, her eyes on Cooper's shirt. She reached out, fingering the torn chambray, her finger tracing the red line beneath the fabric. "I'm not," she smiled. Her own kiss was as intense as the man's. Michael pressed warmly—comfortably—between them. She held on to Cooper's hand after they parted, feeling the strength in his fingers as they wound tightly around her own. As the second horse entered the clearing, she smiled. She reached out with her free hand, gently touching the young woman's leg. "Angela," Regan breathed.

Angela slid off her horse and into Regan's arms. They stood there together, four survivors of a horrible war, locked in the comfort and safety of each other's arms.

*   *   *

Cooper battled four of the confiscated horses into harness as he hitched the stagecoach. His fingers and arms were sore as he struggled with the necessary adjustments on the leather straps, which were stiff with the dried blood of the larger, heavier animals Delgado and his band had slaughtered. Twice he was forced to kick and prod one of the more stubborn horses back to its feet when it lay down in the traces. He yanked at the gelding's ear. "One more time, you sonofabitch," he whispered, "and I'll blow your brains out." As if it understood, the horse scrambled to its feet, immediately complacent.

From somewhere beyond the house, there came the muted rattle and jingle of curb chains and spurs. Cooper paused in his work, searching the darkness for the source of the sound. His jaws tightened when the column of troopers trotted into the yard.

Estevan Folley touched his heels to his mount's flanks, breaking off from the detachment and moving well ahead. He headed for the dim circle of lamplight at the front door, puzzled but inwardly relieved by the waiting coach and the team. The feeling increased tenfold when his friend stepped into the pale glow of the lanterns. "Coop."

Cooper nodded in greeting but said nothing to Estevan, holding his words until the cavalry arrived and their needless ceremony was completed. "Major," he finally drawled.

The officer snapped to attention. "Mr. Dundee." He turned, gesturing toward the rows of troopers with a flamboyant wave of his fringed gloves. "My men are at your disposal, Dundee." He smiled. "And eager for the hunt!"

"Bear?" Cooper smiled. The satire missed its mark, the major's brow knotting. Cooper's face hardened, and he shook his head. "You aren't needed," he said finally. "Not anymore."

The officer was not to be put off. "The hostiles," he

insisted. "The Apache!" He was beginning to feel the fool. An entire company behind him, and no war to fight.

Cooper's patience had reached its limits. "They weren't Apache," he replied tersely. "They were paid killers." He clenched his teeth against a flood of words that he was saving for other ears, struggling to control his temper.

Cooper resumed his chores, finishing the harnessing. He looked at Estevan, not wanting to say more as long as the troopers and their commanding officer remained. When the major rejoined his men, Cooper finally told his friend the rest. "They were mercenaries, Estevan, dressed and armed like Apache. Regan and I took care of them." There was a certain amount of satisfaction in naming the woman, giving her credit.

"All of them," he finished. He slapped the rump of the lead horse as he announced, "I'm going to Tucson." He dug his watch out of his pocket, his fingernail tapping against the crystal. "Plenty of time to deliver the payroll on schedule," he grinned.

Estevan breathed deeply, his eyes narrowing as he recognized his friend's cheerful pretense. "I'll make the ride with you," he said quietly.

Cooper shook his head. "No passengers this trip," he declared flatly. He nodded at the boot. "Just the mail and the payroll." His posture changed slightly as he felt the press of people at his back.

Aaron Beitermann and the other legislators had come out of the house, drawn by the sound of conversation and the louder, restless stamp of the cavalry mounts. The senior legislator bowled his way past Cooper, hurrying to catch up with the army officer, greatly relieved by the man's presence. He pumped the man's hand as if he were afraid to let go.

Estevan slipped past the clutch of men, grabbing Regan's arm as she came out of the house. He pulled her away from the others, keeping his voice low. "Where's Teresa . . . Angela?" he asked, his voice the softest whisper.

Regan's gaze dropped to her hands. "Teresa's dead, Estevan. One of the mercenaries . . ." She reached out, touching his arm. "Coop said it was a man named Delgado. He's dead now, too."

Estevan swore. "Delgado worked for Montgomery. . . ."

Regan failed to conceal her surprise. "Montgomery is the man Jonathan was dealing with, the man who wanted to buy the line. . . ." There was a quiet rustle of muslin and broadcloth as Angela joined them. Regan knew from the look on the young woman's face that she had heard.

"Estevan?" Angela stepped out into the yard, her eyes going wide as she saw the rows and rows of young troopers.

The man's surprise was genuine. He took the girl in his arms, hesitating when he felt her tense beneath his fingers. Wanting to reassure him, she forced a smile and accepted the hug. He touched his lips against her cheek.

Regan touched Angela's sleeve. "I'm going to Tucson with Cooper," she declared. "Would you stay here with Michael?" she asked softly.

The young woman shook her head. "I'm going, too," she breathed. "I think we should *all* go. . . ." Her eyes were on Estevan. She excused herself and disappeared back into the house.

"What do you think we should do, Estevan?" Regan's eyes searched the man's face for answers that were not there.

Estevan shook his head. "I don't know for sure. But one thing *I do* know: Coop's too quiet. He's just too damned quiet. . . ."

The Dundee Transport Line office in Tucson had been built in the early years, before the Anglos came with their red-brick and clapboard siding. Clay-caked strands of aged straw poked from the narrow, flat bricks, whose many layers of whitewash had yellowed from years of exposure to wind and sun. There were only two windows, the old glass thick and imperfect inside rough frames.

Jonathan Dundee was inside, a single lantern casting a yellow pall over the narrow room. The furnishings were not as elegant as the accoutrements of success that dominated the office in Phoenix, but they were sturdy and functional. Most of all, they were familiar—relics from the early days when Malachai had entertained savages and senators with equal aplomb.

Jonathan reached out, absently fingering the desktop carvings that were only partially hidden beneath the tattered blotter. *Jon. Dundee, Esq. 1848.* He would have been six years old.

And Cooper would have been just one.

He'd been thinking a great deal about his half brother in the last few hours—about the look on his face when he had come into the ranch house and saw that Teresa was gone and that Beitermann and the others had done nothing to stop the men who had taken her; about the rage in Cooper's eyes as he measured the men inside the house, and the way that rage turned to a cold indifference after he realized Teresa was gone. His eyes had taken on the dispassionate, wary gleam of a feeding wolf. . . .

The intense soul-searching continued as Jonathan thought about all the things that had happened to him. Like Regan— Regan and her bastard child. His brow knotted as he thought of her, and he experienced a long, childish moment of intense self-pity. From the empty-headed daughters of his associates to the clock-watching whores who pushed watered drinks at the local bordellos, his life had been filled with women who had deceived him. Women—like his mother—who had tried to destroy him.

Except Teresa, he thought guiltily. The one woman who had tried hard to care for him, to win his affection, and he had turned his back on her.

There was a dull, steady ache at his forehead, just above his eyes. He rubbed at the pain, wishing that his mind would rest and allow him peace. But he found no relief.

"Jonathan." Logan Montgomery's voice cut into the dark

silence. He coughed, trying to get the younger man's attention, and then called his name again. When he saw Jonathan raise his head, he continued. "I'm not accustomed to being summoned like some hireling." Without waiting to be asked, he pulled out a chair.

"How long have you been here. In Tucson?" Jonathan asked.

"Long enough," the other smiled. He pulled a long cigar out of his pocket and bit off the end. It took him a while to get the smoke going, and in all that time his eyes never left Jonathan's face. "Did you run into trouble?" he finally asked.

Jonathan returned the speculator's smile. Their usual game of cat and mouse once again. "More trouble than you know, Logan." It was Jonathan's turn to smile. "Your men screwed it up," he breathed. The anger took hold then, and he came forward in his chair, no longer able to play the game. His fist slammed against the desk. "It was Delgado, wasn't it? Delgado and that pack of wolves—"

Montgomery waved his hand, cutting off Jonathan's words. He yawned. There was no point denying it. Not now. "I was tired of waiting, Jonathan." Rising from his chair, he continued, "You've muddled around for a year—trying to convince Coop, trying to persuade the squaw! I made up my mind it had to end! Now!"

"They've taken Teresa!" Jonathan roared. He was on his feet as well. "Goddamn you! They've taken Teresa and Angela as hostages! And the boy!"

"And not your lady friend?" Montgomery mocked. He snorted in disgust. "The old woman was in the way. And as for Angela . . ." He dismissed them with a cold wave of his hand, his cigar leaving a trail of blue-white smoke. "You'll own the majority of Dundee stock when this is over, Jonathan. All of it, if Delgado manages to get Coop as well." The man was talking as if he were reciting details of a cattle trade, his regard for people no greater than his concern would be for slaughterhouse beef. He stared across at Jonathan, surprised that some degree of gratitude didn't show in the man's face. "Did you hear me, man? You'll own it all!"

Jonathan was stunned. Montgomery's real world lay exposed to him for the first time. "You told Delgado to murder her!" Finally he had begun to comprehend everything the man was saying.

"Yes, I told him to kill her!" Montgomery's voice, his face, was filled with contempt. The smile was slow, one corner of his mouth lifting. It was as if he were snarling. "You weak, stupid fool. I thought you had some brains, Jonathan—that you knew what you wanted and had the guts to go after it. *To take it!*"

He was breathless and his face was mottled. "I could understand a delay, a need to try to deal with your family in a softer way than you'd deal with *them*. . . ." He gestured toward the unseen adversaries that existed just beyond the door. "But I didn't think you'd be fool enough to let them stand in the way!"

Jonathan's composure was slowly returning. He ignored the man's rantings. "I want the women returned." The words came with a renewed sense of purpose. "I want Teresa and Angela back!" His fist pumped loudly against the desk.

"Teresa's dead!" Montgomery declared. He laughed. "If I don't know anything else in this world, I know that she's dead!"

Jonathan shook his head. "No . . ." he implored. *"No!"* He lunged forward and grabbed at Montgomery's throat, his hand knotting in the tight thickness at the man's collar. "I'll turn you in, Logan. If Teresa is dead, I'll turn you in. I'll see you hang!" he promised.

"Then we'll hang together," Montgomery retorted. He unwound Jonathan's fingers, pushing the man away. "Think about it, Dundee. You've worked for me, with me, for more than a year now. A little legal work here and there. Some lobbying with your brownnosing friends in Prescott while you promoted my—'' he repeated the word, stressing it ''—*my* railroad.

''And the stage line, Jonathan. You've been shoving it down everyone's throat that you wanted to sell—that you *meant* to sell—to me. Me!'' The cruel smile fired the eyes again. ''Hell,'' he grinned, ''you even tried to convince Malachai. Before his—'' the pause was again intentional ''—his *accident.*''

Jonathan felt as if he had been kicked in the stomach. He had been so damned blind. ''Malachai,'' he breathed.

Montgomery flicked the ash from his cigar onto Jonathan's desk. ''Coop was right, Jonathan. All along. All those months the two of you fought, when Coop was hiding inside a bottle because nobody—because *you*—wouldn't listen, he was right!''

He paused, then went on, ''A loose wheel lug, a stage full of freight—no passengers—a team of horses spooked by a sound they couldn't get away from.'' Montgomery dug into his vest pocket and produced a small leather pouch. He held it up to his ear, shaking it. He shook it harder as he thrust it across the narrow space that separated them.

Instinctively, Jonathan backed up, the harsh dry rattle evoking a primal fear that made him want to run away—just as Malachai's team had run away.

Montgomery dropped the pouch on the desk, glad for the perverse desire that had prompted him to keep it. ''A souvenir,'' he whispered. ''A little something from Delgado . . . to me . . . to you.'' Gingerly, he dumped out the contents of the bag, the collection of snake rattles tumbling across the desk. Such little things, yet they had sent a two-thousand-pound coach and six horses over the side of a high cliff. *And Malachai with them.*

Jonathan felt a surge of pure rage course through him, an anger that pushed away the fear and confusion of only moments before. ''You bastard,'' he breathed. ''You miserable bastard. . .'' He struck out at Montgomery, his fist skimming the man's fat cheek and slamming into the wall. He didn't even feel the pain. He merely swung again.

Cooper's arms ached from the effort of controlling four horses that had never been worked in harness. He seesawed the reins, cursing and shouting at the animals as he drove them on at a full run. They plunged forward into the darkness, white foam flecking their hides as they tried to escape the wheeled demon that pursued them.

Inside the coach, Regan held on to her son, the dog at her feet. She hated the tense silence, wishing that Estevan had ridden inside the coach and not on top. *Even Beitermann and the others would have been better company,* she thought, staring across at Angela. Still, Cooper had been right not to let the lawmakers join them on this ride, and she was glad he had remained adamant in his decision. "The major can have them," he had raged. "He can shove them all up his ass!" That, as far as Cooper was concerned, was the end of it. Major Tyson would have the pleasure of the legislators' company on the long ride home.

Regan tried to read Angela's face. The girl's skin was alabaster beneath the rising moon, her hair spun silver against her pale face. She silently sat staring out the window, rubbing unseen dirt off her arm with one hand while she caressed the folds of her long skirt with the other.

She had changed clothes almost as soon as Cooper had brought her home—changed clothes and bathed even before they had buried her mother. And she, like Michael, had remained so very silent, so very distant.

The heavy yawing eased as the coach began to slow down. Regan could hear the difference as the horses moved across the hard gravel and onto the softer, finer dirt of a more heavily traveled road. The pace continued its gradual slackening, a sideways sway occurring as they negotiated a sharp turn, and then they stopped.

There was a slight, almost imperceivable creak as Cooper

and Estevan left the driver's box; the only other sound was the heavy noise of the team's labored breathing. Regan and Angela waited expectantly, but no one came.

Jonathan's second blow against the land speculator sliced through the air from below, his fist landing solidly in the soft flesh above Montgomery's belt. He kept on at the man, battering his face again and again, forcing him to retreat toward the far wall. Blood and spittle spattered Jonathan's hand and his arm. His own nose was bleeding from Montgomery's few punches, and he tasted the salty warmth in a new flood of wet against his tongue as Montgomery's fist slammed into his chin.

An explosion of sound came from behind them, the noise of the old wooden front door being torn from its hinges. Cooper kicked at the door again, stepping over the threshhold as the heavy wood finally gave. He carried the payroll satchel in one hand; the mail pouch was heavy in the other. He dropped the satchels at Jonathan's feet. "I'm on time, Jonathan. Even ahead of time," he declared.

The room was silent now, the only sound was the slow drag of the brass pendulum on the large wall clock beside Montgomery's head. Cooper's eyes dug into the man, then softened as he slowly swung his gaze to his brother. "Teresa's dead, Jonathan," he whispered. "My mother's dead. . . ." His eye caught a subtle movement as Montgomery's hand stealthily crept across his chest to disappear inside his coat. The big man's face was a study in naked panic.

"It was your brother's fault," he gasped, seeing nothing but death in Coop's yellow-green orbs. "He knew about the whole thing, right from the first. . . ." Desperate, Montgomery's fingers closed around the butt of the small pistol hidden inside his vest.

Cooper said nothing. He raised his left hand to stop the denial that was forming on his brother's lips, his right hand limp at his side. Until Montgomery moved. Cooper waited, watching the sudden lifting of the man's shoulder, and then he drew his own gun. He fired, point-blank, the barrel of the Remington only inches from the man's chest.

"No . . ." Montgomery's weapon tumbled from his fingers, his hands already growing numb. He stared down at his chest, at the growing circle of red staining his shirt, and sagged against the wall. "No . . ." He fell, sliding down the wall and onto his face at Cooper's feet.

Estevan, Regan, and Angela crowded into the doorway, none of them able to move. They watched, horrified, as Cooper turned the gun on his brother.

"No!" Regan's voice broke the stillness. She shouldered her way into the room, mindful of the child who was asleep outside in the coach. "Please, Coop," she begged, her voice soft. She came forward, slowly, her hand extended as she gestured for him to give her the gun. He merely shook his head, keeping the pistol still pointed at Jonathan's gut.

Then, suddenly, he yielded. He was unable to meet the woman's eyes, and for a brief moment he was sorry that he loved her. He tossed the weapon aside, his mouth opening in a wild roar that exploded from deep within him as he lunged at his brother's still form.

They crashed to the floor, arms locked around each other as they rolled and scuffled across the dry planking. For a long while, Jonathan didn't even try to defend himself, and then the feral instinct for self-preservation overwhelmed him, and he began to fight.

There was no stopping them. Both men reverted to the rough and tumble brawling of their youth, only this time it was Cooper who was on top when they stopped rolling across the floor. He straddled his brother, one hand filled with the rich thickness of Jonathan's fair hair as he screwed the man's head around and forced him over onto his belly. His arm closed around Jonathan's neck in a tight stranglehold, the tendons on his forearms standing out as he increased his pressure. Jonathan gagged, his mouth open as he frantically tried to take in more air, his brother's arm effectively cutting off his wind. "Say 'uncle,'" Coop hissed. Then he laughed. It was a hollow sound, without humor, and there was no laughter in his eyes. Just as they were no longer children, and this was not a child's contest.

He stood up, letting go of his brother, his hands shaking as he stepped away from the man. The anger—the hatred—was still a raging fire in the pit of his stomach. Regan reached out to him, but he pulled away. "Get out," he panted. He swung his eyes toward Regan, Estevan, and Angela. "Get out!" he ordered, angry when it was clear they would not.

Jonathan struggled to sit up, his hand massaging his throat, his face gradually returning to its normal hue. He was still gasping for air, his lungs feeling tight and sore inside his empty chest.

Cooper pulled his brother to his feet, dragging him across the floor to the desk. He yanked open the top drawer and pulled out a worn deck of playing cards. He tore away the thick rubber band that bound the deck, releasing Jonathan's arm as he began to shuffle them. "Winner take all," he breathed, his voice unnaturally soft. He slammed the deck down on the desk between them, fanning out the cards in a wide half-circle.

Jonathan stared across at his brother's face, his brow knotting as he tried to read Cooper's eyes. He suppressed the need to smile. It was an old game between them—a game that Jonathan always won. Because the cards were marked; they had always been marked.

This time, however, the stakes were different. "Winner take all," he echoed. The old greed seized him—the terrible need to win. A feeling of shame replaced the avarice when he realized just how much Cooper had already lost. He dropped his gaze, studying the cards. Carefully he read the old codes and made his decision. Pulling out the card with a single finger, he slid it from between the rest.

Cooper's fingers closed around Jonathan's wrist like an iron band. He pulled Delgado's knife from his belt, and pinned the card to the table, certain that Jonathan had tried to cheat him again. His own fingers skimmed through the deck as he quickly searched for the one card with markings he could decipher. Smiling, he picked it up and turned over the ace of hearts. "I know the cards are marked, big brother," he whispered. "I've always known they were marked."

Jonathan nodded. He pulled Delgado's knife free, working the blade loose and using it to flip over the torn card. He had purposely chosen the deuce of clubs. "You won, Coop. . . ." he announced loudly. He held up both cards so Estevan, Regan, and Angela could see.

There was a long silence as Cooper stared into Jonathan's impassive face. Jonathan met his gaze and knew from what he saw that it was too late; the silent apology—the attempt to reconcile their differences—had come too late.

Cooper turned his back on Jonathan. He reached out and touched Angela's sleeve. "We're going home, Angela. You, Regan, Michael, and I are going home." His gentle words were meant as much for Regan as for his sister.

Angela shook her head absently and slipped from beneath his fingers, going to stand beside Jonathan's chair. She placed her hand on his shoulder, opening the folds at the front of her skirt, exposing a pistol. There was the cold sound of metal against metal as she uncocked the piece. "I would have shot you, Coop. If you had used your gun on Jonathan—or if you had really hurt him—I would have shot you. . . ." A single tear rolled down her cheek, the next words coming in a soft, poignant, and apologetic whisper. "I would have killed you."

Cooper's jaw tightened, a great sadness sweeping his face. The pain was evident in his eyes. He was silent for a long time, trying to understand what had happened and unable to reconcile himself to the girl's decision. He had to ask. "Are you sure this is what you want, Angela? That Jonathan is what you want?''

Estevan answered for the girl, sparing her the pain of hurting Cooper more than she already had. "Coop," he murmured, "it's what she's always wanted." Somehow, saying the words helped to ease his own secret torment. He allowed his eyes to caress her for one final time.

Cooper led the others out into the street. He turned to Estevan, both hands reaching out to rest on the man's shoulders. ''Hermano,'' he breathed. *Brother.* The affection he felt for this man far surpassed anything he had ever felt for Jonathan. "I want you to come back to the ranch with us." He was thinking of the man's feelings for Angela—the loss he had suffered—and he longed to comfort him.

Estevan grinned and shook his head. "Not now, Coop." The smile slowly grew, warming his eyes, and he poked a finger against Cooper's chest. "I'll come for the wedding," he announced, winking and nodding his head at Regan.

"You'll be best man!" Cooper promised.

From his office window, Jonathan watched his brother and Estevan share an affectionate, back-thumping farewell, his sense of loss greater than before. Self-consciously, he lifted his arm, feeling at his shoulder for Angela's hand, afraid that she, too, would be gone. He was relieved to feel her fingers close around his own. So much had happened, so much that he didn't understand—anymore than he could understand why the young woman had chosen to stay with him.

He cleared his throat, looking at Montgomery's still form and the wide smear of blood against the wall that marked his downward slide. "There'll be an investigation, Angela. And publicity—a great deal of unpleasant publicity. And I don't have a dime, Angela. Not one damned dime."

She bent forward, kissing his fingertips. "It doesn't matter, Jonathan. The money never mattered."

They left the office together. Arm in arm, they made the

long walk down the deserted boardwalk, the light from the sheriff's office guiding them.

The soft *poof-poof* of the horses' measured plodding sounded in the street ahead of them, the clank and jingle of harness hardware quite loud. The front wheels of the coach pivoted and squealed in protest as Cooper made a tight turn at the end of the street. He urged the team forward, his eyes straight ahead as he pushed them into a gentle trot, the leather reins feeling comfortable and responsive beneath his fingers. He silently thanked the unknown stage-line hostler who had seen to the animals and hitched the fresh team without having to be asked.

Jonathan's step faltered, a hesitancy in him as the coach came toward him. For one brief moment, he and Cooper faced each other. Neither man spoke, their eyes met—collided—then swept away.

Regan was on the seat beside Cooper, with Michael sleeping between them. She half turned, looking over her shoulder at the diminishing figures that were moving off into the growing darkness. "He's still your brother, Coop," she began. There was a gentle censure in her words, her tone. "Talk to him," she urged. There was no response, and she continued, her voice soft and persuasive. "You can't leave like this—without doing something, without trying to help him."

"Watch me," he snapped. The old hardness had returned, and his face was remote, cold. He was stubbornly fighting the need to turn around, to watch Jonathan.

Regan's hands were in her lap, her fingers laced together in a tight ball. No matter what Jonathan had done or had allowed to happen, he didn't deserve this. She had too much respect for his abilities as a manager to believe that everything he had done was designed to serve only his own ambitions. And he was too good a businessman to be forced simply to walk away. "You've taken everything, Coop," she began. "You've left him with nothing. . . ."

Cooper faced her. "He has Angela!" His lips closed in a tight line as he tried to suppress the rage.

"He *needs* you, Coop," she argued. She inhaled, seriously considering each word before she said it. "And you need him."

"Bull!" Coop's single-word reply came with such great intensity that it carried into the night, and he felt Michael stir beside him. Reaching out, he rubbed the boy's neck and soothed him back to sleep. "He's my brother, Regan," he began, and some of the harshness left his voice. "I love him, but I've never really liked him. In all these years, I've never really liked him. And I don't respect him."

The differences between himself and Jonathan seemed as vast and as insurmountable as they had ever been. "He has Angela," he repeated. "And they have Angela's one-third share." He lifted his hand away from the boy and placed it on Regan's shoulder. "A month from now, if not sooner, Jonathan will be back on his feet. He'll be back at the office in Phoenix."

Regan didn't sense the same animosity, the near hatred, she had sensed before, and she was relieved. "And then?" she asked, feeling the need to know.

"He'll fight me for control," Cooper answered. "He'll do his damnedest to take it all back. . . ."

"And you wouldn't have it any other way," she declared, incredulous. She watched his face.

He was smiling, already anticipating the competition. "I wouldn't have it any other way."

★ WAGONS WEST ★

A series of unforgettable books that trace the lives of a dauntless band of pioneering men, women, and children as they brave the hazards of an untamed land in their trek across America. This legendary caravan of people forge a new link in the wilderness. They are Americans from the North and the South, alongside immigrants, Blacks, and Indians, who wage fierce daily battles for survival on this uncompromising journey—each to their private destinies as they fulfill their greatest dreams.